"This is a bad time for our people. Soon, the Cheyenne will know no peace and there will be much trouble for us. I do not know what will happen, but we will be like leaves driven before the wind, and we will be scattered all over the land without a home or a place to camp or hunt. I know these things."

Sun Runner wanted to shout at Old Lodge and ask him why he said these things.

But his heart was stopped, like a dead man's, and the words died in his dry throat. A shadow passed over him and he looked up.

The hawk hovered high above him. And then the golden bird folded its wings and dove straight for him, its talons outstretched. Sun Runner brought his arms up to shield his face and the hawk extended its wings and drenched him in shadow, blocking out the sun for a moment. Just before it struck, Sun Runner closed his eyes. . . .

Tor books by Jory Sherman

Horne's Law
The Medicine Horn
Song of the Cheyenne
Winter of the Wolf

Jory Sherman
Song of the Cheyenne

TOR

A TOM DOHERTY ASSOCIATES BOOK
NEW YORK

This is a work of fiction. All the characters and events portrayed in this book are fictitious, and any resemblance to real people or events is purely coincidental.

SONG OF THE CHEYENNE

Copyright © 1987 by Jory Sherman

All rights reserved, including the right to reproduce this book, or portions thereof, in any form.

A Tor Book
Published by Tom Doherty Associates, Inc.
175 Fifth Avenue
New York, N.Y. 10010

Tor ® is a registered trademark of Tom Doherty Associates, Inc.

ISBN: 0-812-53095-0
Library of Congress Catalog Card Number: 86-29245

First Tor edition: January 1989

Printed in the United States of America

0 9 8 7 6 5 4 3 2

This one's for Ray Puechner, with thanks . . .

After the question of providing subsistence for himself and his family, the main thing that occupied the mind of the Cheyenne was the protection of his people from the attacks of enemies and the effort to reduce the power of these enemies by attacks on them.

The fighting spirit was encouraged. In no way could a young man gain so much credit as by the exhibition of courage. Boys and youths were trained to feel that the most important thing in life was to be brave; that death was not a thing to be avoided; that, in fact, it was better for a man to be killed while in his full vigor rather than to wait until his prime was past, his powers were failing, and he could no longer achieve those feats which to all seemed so desirable.

George Bird Grinnell
The Fighting Cheyennes

PROLOGUE

I speak of wars and the ways of warriors. I speak of the people, the *Tsis-tsis-tas* and the *Suh-tai*, those of us called by our friends, the Lakota, *Sha-hi-e-na*, and by the white men Cheyennes. I speak of the great warrior, *Wo-iv-sto-is*, which means Alights On The Cloud in the white man's tongue. This one was called Iron Shirt by the Skidi Pawnees and he was killed by one of their medicine people and this was the time when one of our young men became more famous than even Iron Shirt.

I speak of the troubles that came to our people in those days when the buffalo hat was sacred and when we had the medicine arrows. I believe our people's troubles began when there was disrespect shown to the buffalo hat and when we had the great fight with the Skidi Pawnees and Iron Shirt was killed by one of the enemies' medicine men.

The young man of whom I speak, who was there when Iron Shirt was killed, was the strange one of the tribe. His father was a Northern Cheyenne, his mother of the Southern tribe. As a boy, he was called Eats-Meat-Quickly, but in a terrible fight with the Crow people, when he was no more than a shadow in size, when his bones showed through his chest skin and his hair had not grown out long and black, his magic and his personal medicine brought him another name. This was to be a great name in our two tribes, but no one knew it at the time. We only knew that the name had much power and truth in it, and we who were there at the Crow fight knew that the Great Power had to be watching over such a one.

For a long time, this brave warrior was never spoken of outside the tribe and many of his adventures were held secret because he was a quiet man not given to bragging and many of us thought that his medicine was so strong that to tell about him would break his magic. Maybe that is what happened, in the end, but there are those of our people alive today who say that this young man, this bravest of warriors, is alive today and that he will never die.

There are some, too, who think that his spirit still walks the old lands, that it dwells on the Upper Missouri and sojourns to the beloved Smokey Hill country where his mother's people loved to hunt, and where he himself killed many buffalo, fought the Snake people and the white men.

His story has been handed down these many seasons and now that all who knew him are spirits who have gone to the sky, it is said that we can talk of him and his medicine. But I do not think the people talk of him too much, even so. He lived in another time when our people were different, when they still followed the old ways, and they were the bravest people of the plains and of the mountains. He lived among us and maybe lives among us still, under a different name. I do not know the truth of these imagined things. I do know the truth of this story, for I am Woven Rug, the grandson of

Alights On The Cloud, who was called Iron Shirt by the Skidi Pawnee who killed him, killed his magic.

The song I sing here is of another, the young man once called Eats-Meat-Quickly until he grew into a man. This man of my song is the one who must be remembered because he never lost his magic or his medicine.

The one I sing of is Sun Runner, whose name has much meaning even today, long after Sand Creek, the Washita, Wounded Knee, and the Little Big Horn.

This is the story of Sun Runner. This is his song.

CHAPTER ONE

Corn Woman clucked her tongue against the roof of her mouth, making sounds like the prairie hen that chases its chicks into the brush when the sniffing coyote tracks her spoor on the dew-beaded prairie grasses. She sat with her people, the Suh-tai, the "people left behind," in their camp circle outside the big circle, the third circle from the opening in the east, where the sun came back, brought life and power to all the people. She worked the buckskin in her hands, wadding it up, stretching it, shining it across a small tree stump in her lap to take out the stiffness, make it soft. She watched her son, Eats-Meat-Quickly, as he skulked among the lodges of the *Hev-a-tan-iu,* the Hair-rope people, two circles away. Her eyes clouded with the proud shadows that fill a mother's eyes when her son grows straight and tall as a lodgepole pine, begins to show muscles in his legs like the deer, in his arms like the sleek ripples under a panther's skin.

Ah, but her son was so quiet and quick, as he hid from the other boys, ran from them, wild as any yearling colt. Her chest swelled to see him there in the shadow of Burning Knife's old squirrel-gnawed lodge, his long, lean legs bent under him like the rabbit's, ready to spring at the first sign of danger. The buckskin in her hands seemed to take on life as she kneaded it with deft brown fingers, pulled on it until it was taut as a drumhead, then let it crumple into a wad of wrinkled leather. This would make a fine shirt for her son and she imagined him wearing it, strutting among the lodges like a warrior with fresh Pawnee scalps on his lance.

A boy from one of the lodges in the *Hof-no-wa*, the poor people's circle, sneaked around Burning Knife's lodge, came up behind Eats-Meat-Quickly. Corn Woman's heart beat faster as though she were part of the game, feared for her son's capture. She glanced away a moment, as if afraid for this feeling to show on her face, and she drew a deep breath into her lungs, let it out slow that it would not become a sigh. Her aunt, Wool Woman, smiled at her with crooked teeth, the wrinkles stretching with her distended lips until she looked as if she had been drinking the juice of fermented grain. When Corn Woman looked back toward her son a scant stretch of the sun-stick's shadow later, Eats-Meat-Quickly was gone and the stalking boy from the poor people's camp was scratching his head, looking all around as if her son had been swallowed by the earth.

Corn Woman laughed, and the sigh that was in her came out anyway, like a wind that springs up cool when it is hot under the sun and makes the lodge comfortable, blows out all the dead-still air.

Wool Woman sat before the small fire, dipping the horn spoon in the boiling water to soften it, give it shape. She looked at Corn Woman for a long moment, her lips twisted in that crooked, wrinkled smile, her eyes aflash with light, looking like bright beads shining with captured sunlight. Wool Woman appeared dark against the white of her renewed lodge, but she sat in its shadow, small, her jagged teeth carious from age and neglect, her fingers shaping the handle of the horn spoon as though independent of her body, her arms.

"He becomes a man, soon," Wool Woman said, her voice a rasp in her throat, high-pitched like the terrified bark of a gray squirrel startled in the deep woods.

"Tomorrow he goes with the men," replied Corn Woman.

"He will bring you horses."

"Bear Heart will watch after him . . ." She made a show of biting her tongue, thrusting it between her teeth, flapping her lips closed. The hide crackled in her hands, popped as she drew it taut, twisted it like a wet rag.

Wool Woman's eyes narrowed, trapped the light, squeezed it to an awl-point until each eye projected but a single tiny beam.

"Ahhh," she said, "you do not want him to grow to a man."

"I did not say such."

"This old woman sees the way you watch your child and knows your nipples hurt on your breasts as if they still were fat with milk. Eats-Meat-Quickly is already tall and you must let him be a man. He will bring you much honor when he comes back with horses."

Corn Woman sucked saliva through the gaps in her teeth so that they made sounds like insects working their mandibles, feeding on corn or wheat, or rubbing their saw-toothed legs together in concert. She looked off beyond the smoke-smudged wing flaps of the lodges, into the clear blue bowl of the sky, and thought about her son. She thought about him deeper than she ever had before, seeing him wiry as a strong, tough weed that grew in hard earth, and seeing him grow beyond that into the sky like a tall green tree. She saw him in her mind as she had seen him that morning, practicing with the bow, as if to draw the eyes of the young girls to him and the young boys, too, throwing arrows as if they were red thunderbolts with feathers, playing a wheel game, and sliding his throwing stick along the ground until it scuffed up dust, slid slow to its stop at the finger-drawn line that was the target.

In the empty of a sky the color of a redchested bird's egg, she saw the thinking pictures behind her eyes, the lodge where she had swelled up with her son inside her belly, up on the river in the sacred hills of the Lakota. She began to make the sounds with her teeth and mouth that were like the throaty husks of quail or prairie chickens when they mated, and her nipples surged and pained with a distant hurt that was only memory, the thinking pictures that had gone away for many seasons.

When her son was born, on the Cheyenne River, in *Ok-sey-e-shi-his*, the Hoop-and-Stick Game Moon, they called him *Mok-so-is*, Pot Belly, because he was boy and his nature was sweet as the syrup paste made by the white man's fly, the bee that made its nests in the tree hollows. Because it was cold, and there was snow on the ground, she wrapped him with soft deerskin and marten fur to keep him warm. For three moons she carried him around in her arms, instead of in a cradleboard, because he was frail like the young buffalo calf. She held him close to her so that he could hear her heart beat with love for him, and so he could easily drink of her milk when he had hunger. His father, Bear Heart, often played with him in the lodge, letting him try to grasp the arrow shaft in his tiny hand, or pull at his braids. He rubbed his nose against the boy's, mashing it like a berry, laughing at the funny face little Pot Belly made. She was glad the people did not move out on the prairie that season because many babies died in the cold winds from the north at such times and she did not want her son's spirit to be taken away.

When he grew hardy, she let him see the snow and feel the cold wind until he shivered, but then she would bundle him up again and take him into the lodge, rock with him by the fire while he suckled and made the baby noises of contentment. She made the child a toy rattle from the sac of a male antelope, filled it with dried piñon nuts, sewed it together with sinew. She could still see the thinking pictures of him smiling, toothless, as he shook the rattle, listened to the piñon nuts clattering together. Bear Heart let the boy chew on his finger, after he smeared it with grease, then laughed as the child wrinkled up its face and spat the finger from its puckered mouth.

Corn Woman chuckled to think of these old, almost forgotten things. She sobered when she thought of the first time she put him in the cradleboard. He kicked and fought, held his breath until his lips turned purple as the dusk sky. When she walked, though, his fierce anger turned to joy and he bobbed there on her back, looking around him and down at her, laughing when she turned to look back up at him before quickly turning away as if hiding. He stayed in the board most of the time, so she could work, keep the lodge clean, cook the food for her husband. She sometimes hung him up on a lodgepole, or leaned him against the hide so that he could play with his rattle and watch her bustle about. When she let him play on the ground, he was like a little animal. He could move fast, too, and always got into things that were dangerous. He tasted the things of the earth at such times: grass, dirt, pebbles, insects, pulled them up to his mouth in a tiny fist, looking at her wide-eyed as if daring her to take away his treasures. When the tribe moved, he traveled on her back, or sometimes she would turn him around so that he faced her. When he fell asleep, his head bobbed like a doll's and when he was awake, she fed him bits of food as they walked along, or played the teasing game with him, where she would hide her face or look away quickly whenever their eyes met.

When little Pot Belly was three moons of age, during *Pun-u-ma-es-si-ni*, the Light Snow Moon, Corn Woman took him to the Medicine Lodge to have his ears pierced. Bear Heart asked the old crier, Lame Mule, to call out for one who would pierce the boy's ears.

"Who will you have do this thing?" asked Lame Mule.

"Ho-nuhk-ka-wo," said her husband, and many who were there made noises with their mouths and shook their heads or dug fingers in their ears as if they were stopped up with wax. For the name he had spoken was that of Lightning Lance, who was a Contrary. He was a very old man, but a Contrary, and he carried such a lance with him everywhere he went. It was shaped like a bow and strung with sinew, but one end of it bore the chipped flint of a lance and the feathers of war birds danced beneath the spearhead when he walked about.

"Why do you call him?" she asked her husband.

"Because the boy is uncommon," replied Bear Heart, "and the medicine of Lightning Lance is very strong."

Those who heard him nodded, but there were some who said the boy would grow up crazy or contrary if Ho-nuhk-ka-wo performed this ceremony. Corn Woman smiled now, because she was one of those who thought Bear Heart's mind was cloudy, like what some called that same moon, *Shi-iv-i-ne,* Dusty Moon, that the white man calls March.

The crier called out for Lightning Lance and the old man came up carrying his contrary weapon. Bear Heart asked him to pierce the ears of little Pot Belly.

"You do not want Lightning Lance to do this," said the old warrior.

"No," said Bear Heart.

Lightning Lance smiled crooked as a hunting snake and turned his back on Bear Heart.

"I will not do this thing," he said, and drew his sharp-pointed flint knife from his sash. He hurled his bow-lance to the ground, snatched the baby from Corn Woman's arms, and began to chant.

"I will not count coup," said the Contrary. "I will not tell of the time when the *Shi-shi-ni-wi-he-tan-iu,* the snake men (the people the white men call Comanches), came back to the Black Hills for scalps. I will not tell how they killed Running Crow and Blue Weasel before the sun awoke and we could find our weapons. I will not tell how brave I was, knocking one of them down and stealing his horse. I will not say how many snake men I knocked down, but the sand and the grasses were red with blood and I will not say that I killed two snake men with my war club and broke it inside an enemy's brains so that they all ran off like screeching children when the bear comes out of its cave above the berry thicket. And I will not pierce the ears of this little baby."

At first, Corn Woman thought that Lightning Lance would wave his hands over the boy's ears and make gestures with the flint knife, so that someone else could do it after this sacred time. But the tall, lean Contrary, with the face as sharp as a chipped flint ax, rammed the point of his knife into first one ear lobe and then the other. His hands were like shadows that blurred through tears.

It happened so fast, no one was prepared for Lightning Lance to do this thing.

The boy did not even whimper. Instead, she recalled, he threw up his arms as if to fight the Contrary. Lightning Lance jumped backward as if afraid, and stood there, shaking like the thin aspen when the wind comes up quick.

Bear Heart let out a shout of triumph as the blood oozed from the boy's earlobes. Pot Belly slapped at his ears as if at mosquitoes and everyone laughed to see how brave he was. Corn Woman beamed, until her husband spoke to the Contrary.

"For this," he said, "I give you three horses!"

Corn Woman gasped at the wonder of this. One horse would have been enough for such a deed.

"I will not take them," said Lightning Lance, holding out his hand.

Her son dashed by her at that moment (interrupting her reverie), fleet as a deer, and his arm flashed outward from his body. Something dropped from his hand, fell into her lap.

Corn Woman looked up, saw his teeth grow white as his lips peeled back in a boyish grin.

And, then, he was gone again, racing toward the far lodges, two other boys in hot pursuit.

She looked down in her lap, saw the blue-petaled mountain flower.

"Yes," she murmured to herself, "he is a good, strong son. He will make a brave warrior."

She remembered, too, when Bear Heart gave the boy his name and a horse. He took the boy in his arms, held him in front of the pony he would not be able to ride for two or three snows, spoke the words *Na-vi-hisht-nat-a-mit*, "My name I give to him," and gave him his own name because there was no uncle who sent for the child to give him his name. After young Bear Heart's ears were pierced, the pony was given away. He was, by then, called Bear-Eats-Meat-Quickly because he had the appetite of a young bear waking up from winter sleep. This name was shortened to Eats-Meat-Quickly and some had even forgotten his real name.

The boy learned his lessons well. He learned to stay quiet so that he did not disturb the old ones in the lodge, or make noise on the trail. His father gave him a bow to play with and taught him how to hold onto the horse's mane when they rode. Eats-Meat-Quickly learned to ride much sooner than anyone expected. He had good balance, and he was not afraid, but that was because he first rode the old pack-ponies and these were gentle and docile, unlike the war-ponies. After his ears were pierced, he began to ride the young colts bareback, and soon he joined the other boys who tended the horses in the hills. There, he learned how to handle the rope. Corn Woman remembered how proud Bear Heart was to see his son throw the rope and catch the horse her husband wanted to ride, sneaking up close, making the loop, and hurling it through the air. The loop dropped around the horse's neck and the boy dug in his bare heels, taking up the slack when the horse tried to run away.

These thoughts evaporated—like the dew on morning grasses when the sun wakes and burns the land—as Corn Woman heard a cry beyond the circle and stiffened. She started to put down the deerskin and run to see what had happened.

Wool Woman shook her head.

"That was Eats-Meat-Quickly," said Corn Woman. "Maybe he has been hurt."

"The other boys have caught him. Maybe they want to teach him a lesson."

Corn Woman glowered. Her eyes glittered like the eyes of a mother buffalo when her calf is threatened. But, she sat still, knowing the old woman was right. The boy was soon to be a man.

"Maybe he will teach them a lesson," she muttered. "Bad boys."

Wool Woman laughed softly.

A moment later the two women both heard the pound of pony hooves, the small thunders that set the dogs to barking and the other children to screaming. She looked at Wool Woman in desperation, trying to hide the sudden fear that rose up in her chest and throttled her like a squeezing hand.

No, her son had not screamed because of the boys, but because he had been the first to see the scouts. In that cry of joy, he had put a dart into her heart and she wished it had been only hurt so that she could tend to him, soothe him one last time—or keep him from going with the braves.

It seemed, then, as if the thunder of pony hooves was very loud and the sound had clogged her ears until she could only hear them muffled as though they were far away. She heard the excited voices, the deep boom of the braves talking in excitement, and the women and children shouting until she could not stand it any longer and threw down the rag of deerskin and stood up on shaky moccasined feet. Then, as if wax had been dug from her ears, the sounds were very loud and she saw her son running toward her, his short black hair whipping in the wind he made with his running. She heard him yelling at her so loud that she wished she could not hear. She wished she could put the words back in his mouth so she could not hear them.

"They came for the medicine pipes!" he shouted. "They have found horses! There will be fighting!"

She opened her mouth to speak, but her voice caught in her throat like a bird tangled in a thorn thicket, and Eats-Meat-Quickly flashed by her like a tawn deer and disappeared inside the lodge. His face was smudged with dirt and his skin streaked with little rivers of sweat. That was all she could think of, then, as she drew in a quick, sharp breath to shake off the giddiness.

The boy emerged from the lodge with his bow and his quiver bristling with arrows. The thongs of his medicine bundle looped over his sash, flopped against his breechclout. Corn Woman thought that he did not look old enough to make war.

"We are going on foot," he said to her, his face abeam with an inner light. "I am going to the sweat lodge and to see the medicine arrows."

She reached out for him, but he dodged her and dashed away, his rump flapping with the tail end of his breechclout. Only the image of his dark eyes remained crystal in her memory after he disappeared in the forest of conical lodges.

"Sit," said Wool Woman softly. "They will go soon, bring back many horses."

As if in a trance, Corn Woman sank slowly to the ground.

"Yes," she muttered, "my little boy will never return."

"Eh?" asked the old woman with the bowl.

"My life is full," said Corn Woman, and there was pride in her voice. "I have seen my boy for the last time."

He would not return, she knew.

Instead, a man would come back from battle, and she would not know who he was. He would have a new name and would be only with men until he took a wife.

And she was proud and she could still see his eyes in her mind, so bright and shining, brown as the swelling cottonwood buds. A boy's eyes no more, but a man's, full of the light that shines in a warrior's heart, fiercer than any sun, more dazzling than any white winter's moon.

Corn Woman picked up the hank of buckskin and began kneading it, kneading it slow in her quivering hands.

CHAPTER TWO

Eats-Meat-Quickly ran fleet to the place where the scouts gathered. A crowd of men and boys stood in a respectful semicircle around the braves who had ridden in search of horses. He saw Rope Earrings, his body sleek with sweat, his brown eyes shining like bright beads, talking to Lame Medicine, his hands flying like birds as he made sign, his talk full of powerful grunts and hisses like the puff adder makes when it is frightened.

Rope Earrings was the oldest of those who had gone to find the ponies and he wore an old flint arrowpoint tied to his scalp lock. He wore this, it was said, because his dream had told him to do this, and many thought the arrowpoint was big medicine from long ago times given to him by some spirit.

The boy stood on the balls of his feet, pressed against the back of Little Wolf to hear what the warrior was saying.

"There are many horses," Rope Earrings said. "Many fine Crows. On the river. We saw them, counted one hundred horses, thirty Crows. I wish to make war, capture the horses. I ask permission of Medicine Snake to lead the war party. I ask that two young boys carry the medicine arrows and the sacred hat."

Eats-Meat-Quickly sucked in his breath. A swarm of

night moths swirled in his stomach and he looked down at his legs to see if they were quivering with the excitement he felt inside him. He knew this must be an important attack on their old enemies the Crow. He looked around him and did not see that many warriors, for most of the others were scouting for buffalo and would be gone for many suns. There were thirty Crow on the river and no more than a dozen Cheyennes to go against them. Many of these were old—Rope Earrings himself had seen nearly forty winters. Some were boys, like himself, most of them older. He saw Spotted Dog there, with his brother, Running Elk, and Red Tracks, the son of Thunder Wind, who did not like any of the younger boys.

"Who are these boys?" asked Lame Medicine.

Some of the boys shouted, "Me, me, pick me." And they crowded in, pushed this way and shoved that way with their elbows and shoulders until Thunder Wind glowered at them with a dark face that puffed up like a stormcloud.

"I will look them over," said Rope Earrings. "They must be good, strong, brave boys."

Eats-Meat-Quickly saw Red Tracks push Spotted Dog aside and step into the circle with the men. His father, Thunder Wind, strode to the young man's side, stood by him, moccasin to moccasin. Eats-Meat-Quickly felt his heart shrink in his chest and the bottom fell out of his stomach. He felt very small, like a stump left by the gnawing beaver while the flowering tree floats away dead on the waters of the stream.

Rope Earrings looked at the young brave, and at the other boys peering at him from the edge of the packed circle. He waved his arms, pushing his palms outward toward the circle. In sign, he told them all to move back, to give him more room so he could pick out the two boys he wanted to carry the sacred hat and the medicine arrows.

"Let all the boys come to me," he growled. "Let me see how strong they are. You, there, small boy, come out here where I can look at your legs and your muscles."

Some of the boys tittered like chuckling quail because Rope Earrings pointed to a very small boy who was called Yellow Throat. The boy had a dozen winters, but he was small and thin as a reed.

"And you, and you," the brave commanded, and the boys began to emerge from the circle and step cautiously away from the edge. Eats-Meat-Quickly hung back, because Red Tracks still glared at him, and he was so menacing, Eats-Meat could not look into his fierce dark eyes.

Then, Red Tracks stepped forward, stood among the young boys. He thrust out his chest and drew himself up tall. His black braids hung straight down his lean back, the tips tied with leather strips strung through snail shells. He folded his arms across his midsection.

Rope Earrings looked around at the gathering, then pointed to Eats-Meat-Quickly.

"You there, boy," he said sharply. "Why do you stand there? Are you not Bear Heart's son?"

The boy nodded, struck mute by the sudden attention. He felt the looks of others burning into him. His face grew hot as if a firewind had struck him, and blood rose up from his neck until he thought it would blow out through his ears.

"Step close," said the warrior. "Come, come, don't shy back like a young colt."

Laughter rippled from the throats of the men and boys, and Eats-Meat-Quickly saw the toothy grins of his friends. Red Tracks was the only one who did not laugh. He summoned the courage to step into the circle, trod forward on trembling legs.

He stood there, quivering inside, as Rope Earrings looked him over, exaggerating his movements. He circled the boy, looked him up and down as the others suppressed chuckles that bubbled beneath their breaths.

"He is not very big yet," said the warrior. "But he has the legs of a young antelope. His hair is short, so no Crow would want his scalplock."

The men laughed then, and the boys echoed the laughter in chorus as if glad to see someone else take the tickling, relieved to let out the laughs and cover their own nervousness.

"Can you run fast, boy? Can you dance? Are you afraid of the Crow?"

"Y—yes, ah, yes, no, I don't know," Eats-Meat stammered. His face flushed a dark crimson and he looked hard at the ground, at Rope Earrings' beaded moccasins.

"Dance," said Rope Earrings.

"Dance?"

"Dance as if we were all Crow here waiting to cut off your head and put it in the boiling pot."

Confused, the boy looked around at the others. There was no laughter now, only stern, stolid faces floating through a mist, and his friends seemed to draw away, their faces blank as stone.

He saw his father, Bear Heart, standing behind Thunder Wind and there was no expression on his face either. But he saw something in his father's eyes, a shining like a smooth stone at the bottom of a stream and he drew courage from that quick look. He moved his leaden feet, slowly at first, picking first one up, then the other. They were heavy as iron and then they turned light. He lifted them higher and then he was floating, dancing in a circle, and his voice, or someone else's voice, rose out of his throat in a chant like those war songs he had heard the men sing ever since he could remember. Around and around he danced, faster and faster, until faces were a blur and blended into one another like falling leaves in autumn and his voice grew stronger until he could feel his own fierceness boiling in his blood, surging through his veins, swelling his heart.

Faster and faster he whirled until he was dizzy, light-headed, and his voice began to fade as his heart pumped until he could hear it roaring in his ears like the beating wings of an eagle. He stopped, his head still whirling, and looked at Rope Earrings, his lips twisted in a half-smile. His arms hung limp at his sides and his chest muscles rippled as his lungs swelled with deep gulps of air.

There was a silence among those in the circle, and the young boys shifted weight on their feet, but made no sound. Eats-Meat batted his eyes closed like a sleepy owl, as his chest heaved and sweat oiled his skin until it shone like an otter's.

"This one will carry the medicine arrows," said Rope

Earrings, "and he can choose the boy who will bear the sacred buffalo hat."

Red Tracks sucked in a breath, opened his mouth as if to shout a protest. Instead, he fixed Eats-Meat with a look of hatred that was like a storm gathering strong winds and building black clouds in the hills. He clenched his fists at his side, and closed his mouth fast and final as a snapping turtle's on a crayfish.

Eats-Meat saw the look and turned his gaze away from Red Tracks' dark look. Rope Earrings started to rock on his heels, made a sign with one hand that told the boy he should speak.

"Who will you name, young man?" asked the warrior.

Eats-Meat looked around at the other boys, saw the beseeching looks in their eyes. He knew that each of them wanted the honor of carrying the buffalo hat into battle, and whichever ones he passed over would have bad hearts toward him. He knew that Red Tracks wanted to be the one, more than any of the others, but he did not like the older boy, and he did not trust him.

"I choose Spotted Dog," he said quickly, pointing to his friend.

"That little one?"

"Yes."

Rope Earrings grinned. He stepped over to Eats-Meat and patted him on the top of his head.

"This is good," he said. "You have a good heart. Let it be done." He drew himself up tall and looked at the assemblage. "We have the bearers of the medicine arrows and the sacred buffalo hat. They are small and we will make medicine so they will be invisible to the enemy. They will carry these holy things into battle and we will bring back many Crow horses."

"Hou, hou," the men cried. *"Ha ho!"* they chorused.

"Now, I ask Old Lodge to talk to the spirits, and bless the sacred pipe and the medicine arrows and the buffalo hat, for we set out before the next sun wakes up for the Crow camp."

Spotted Dog raced to Eats-Meat's side, slapped him on the shoulder. He jumped up and down as if he had held his water too long. He made such a fool of himself that Eats-Meat wanted to kick him.

"What now? What now, big brother?" Spotted Dog asked, so excited his words came out of his mouth in pieces as if they were broken off and spit out on separate breaths.

"I do not know, I do not know," said Eats-Meat and then realized he was as excited as Spotted Dog and just as confused.

Bear Heart appeared beside them, and hunched down to whisper-talk to them.

"You will go to the house of Old Lodge and listen to the blessing of the sacred things and he will tell you what the spirits say. Be little men and be silent. This is a great honor, my son, and Bear Heart has much pride that Rope Earrings has chosen you to carry the medicine arrows."

"You will not come to the lodge of Old Lodge?" Eats-Meat asked.

"No. I go to prepare for the next sun."

"You will go with us to steal the Crow horses?"

"Yes. I will see my son become a man."

Eats-Meat stood there for a long moment, the pride in him beating like wardrums in his ears. The trembling inside him had gone away.

CHAPTER THREE

Red Tracks stood in the shadow of a lodge at the edge of the clearing. He watched Eats-Meat-Quickly, with narrowed, hate-slitted eyes. He rubbed a thumb down his bare belly, streaking the sweat into a line, a muddy smear of dirt. A look of cunning played like summer shadows across his aquiline face.

"Psst!" he called.

Eats-Meat's head jerked up. He looked around, saw the faint outline of Red Tracks next to the lodge.

"You want me?" he asked warily.

"Yes. Come. I want to show you something."

"What is this? I see no thing in your hand."

"The horses. I want to show you a fine pony that I might give you."

Eats-Meat felt his stomach swirl with invisible wings. He took a step toward Red Tracks, then stopped. He did not trust this boy. Yet, the promise of a pony made his senses prickle with interest.

"Why do you do this?" he asked the older boy.

"Maybe we can trade."

"I have no thing to trade."

"Come. Let us look at this fine pony."

Red Tracks turned his naked back on Eats-Meat. The shoulder blades stretched the iron-earth-colored skin taut as a drumhead, and Eats-Meat could see the little bones of his spine wrinkling the skin. The tall youth walked away, toward the slope where the ponies grazed. He did not look back. Eats-Meat hesitated for the barest movement of the sun, then broke into a trot, chasing after the older boy.

He fell into step beside Red Tracks, then looked back at the camp with its circles of lodges all shining white as bone in the sun. It seemed so far away now and no one looked their way. He looked at the lazy curls of smoke that rose from the smokeholes of some lodges and felt a tug of lodge sickness that made him ashamed. He heard the faraway voices of small children still playing, the sharp whack of their sticks clacking together like teeth bones, the thunk of wood against hide balls, and the sinewy yaps of dogs, the low murmur of voices that sounded like spirits, or the wind roaming through small trees in the high rock places of mountains. His stomach still wriggled with the flutter of unseen insects but he did not know if this was fear or excitement over the pony. He wondered if Red Tracks had a bad heart toward him over what had happened with Rope Earrings and Spotted Dog. He looked at Red Tracks' face and did not see anger there. The fluttering in his belly began to lessen.

Ponies whickered as the two boys approached. He saw some of the horses buck and run as their tails flapped at flies. His ears filled with the sounds of the hills, the faint breeze rustling the grasses, the meadowlarks trilling with the shrill tongues of happy girls, the incessant leg-rub and groan-buzz of insects. His bare feet made sounds, too, and bent the grasses, winced at small stones, curled at the good-feeling caress of soft earth.

The trees above the pony herd, cedars and spruce and pines, made sounds that he could barely hear, and their silhouettes bristled with the paint splotches of yellow and purple and blue and red flowers. The ponies, too, looked painted on the hillside and he thrilled to their iron-colored and berry-blotch patterns sprinkled among the stone-toned and black-rock hides of the big war-horses. He smelled their scents and felt his blood run hot to jump on their long, bony backs and ride to battle with his face streak-smeared for war, his hair long and flying in the wind, his bow strung and arrows in his hand, the flints chipped sharp and hard as a beaver's tooth.

"Where is the pony?" Eats-Meat asked when he saw that Red Tracks had gone beyond the pony herd and into the fringe of the trees above the gentle grazing slope.

"Umm. There," said Tracks, "in the flat place where the little stream runs."

Eats-Meat turned, extended his right arm, pointed a finger downslope toward the pony herd.

"That is the pony. . . ."

He heard the muffled whump-whump of moccasins pounding on the ground, the sound getting louder. At first he did not know that they were made by Red Tracks. He started to turn, when he felt something slam hard into his side. His legs flew out from under him and the breath in his lungs blew out in a sudden rush. He struck the ground, gasping. Strong arms clasped him, rolled him over. He looked up into the dark hawk face

of Red Tracks, saw his head wobble as if watching it
from under water. Tears leaked from his eyes, un-
wanted tears of pain and surprise.

Red Tracks began to strike the younger boy, hitting
him on the head with doubled-up fists. Red Tracks'
mouth drew up until his lips were pinched together like
a hide pouch with the drawthong pulled taut.

"Stop, stop!" Eats-Meat cried.

"Bad boy. Shame, shame. I strike, I strike. You piece
of filth. You dog-grunt bad boy." The words came out
chopped, in his anger, a stream of them that stung like
lashes of wet hide fringes.

Dark spots danced in Eats-Meat's brain and white
sparks like ball lightning flashed in the blackness.

Red Tracks pulled the hair of the youth beneath his
straddling legs, jerked out tufts of black hairs.

Eats-Meat struggled, heaved to unseat the heavier
boy. He rolled and felt a blow glance off his cheekbone
with the force of a stone. His movement carried him
out from under Red Tracks. Eats-Meat scrambled to his
feet.

Fear rose up in his throat, closed it tight. He watched
as the bigger boy stood up, shook himself, then charged,
his head lowered like a fighting elk's.

Eats-Meat sidestepped, quick as a cougar and Red
Tracks whipped past him, his momentum hurling him
off-balance so that he stumbled, sprawled headlong in
the grasses, smearing them flat as he slid. Angered, he
whirled around, squatted on quivering legs.

"Bad face," he snarled. "Bad face ugly boy."

Eats-Meat's side ached, and he panted for breath, his
lungs full of hot coals.

"Why do you talk hate to me?" he gasped.

"You—you are not one to carry the sacred arrows. You bad face."

Eats-Meat saw the hatred in Red Tracks' eyes, saw them narrow and grow dark as the sap that leaks from pines in spring, glittering in the sunlight like amber beads. He knew now why he had been tricked into coming to this place, why Red Tracks wanted to fight him, to beat him so that he could not carry the sacred arrows when they went after the Crow.

The younger boy stiffened, a rage inside him knotting his stomach, building like a stormcloud until it seethed and smoked, swelled out the blood-cords in his neck, hardened his muscles, swept away his fear of the older boy.

"No!" Eats-Meat yelled. "You will not do this." He ran toward Red Tracks, then, faster than he had ever run before. All reason left him so that he was blinded and the hatred spilled out of him, yet left him strong and unafraid. He saw the look of surprise on Red Tracks' face and he flew into him, his arms churning like the wings of prairie swifts. He flailed and felt his fists strike bone and flesh as he crashed into Red Tracks. A deep feeling of satisfaction rose up in him as he knocked the boy backward, kept socking him and smashing him until his breath whistled through his throat and nose and his chest heaved with the struggle to breathe.

Red Tracks lifted his arms to ward off the blows, but Eats-Meat smashed through them and laughed inside when he saw the older boy's nose explode blood, spray his bare chest until it was crimson. Red Tracks cried out and Eats-Meat struck him again, knocked him down to his knees.

"Enough, enough," screamed the older boy. "I have blood. I am sick."

Eats-Meat kicked him in the stomach, saw the youth crumple, fall to his side. Red Tracks drew his legs up and tried to hide his face. He looked like a big porcupine without quills, all balled up, crying like a baby, his nose gushing blood.

Eats-Meat stood over Red Tracks for a long time, drawing in precious breath to drown the fires in his lungs. He gloated, his lips cracked in an insane smile, his chest swelling bigger with each lungful of air. Finally, Red Tracks stopped sobbing and pleading and just lay there, drawn up like one with a stomachache, and whimpered.

Eats-Meat spit on him and walked away, the ache in his side gone, his moccasins just barely touching the ground, floating down the hillside, through the pony herd, feeling above them, above the camp, weightless as a quail feather. It was good, this thing that had happened. It made him feel good inside that he had beaten Red Tracks, had drawn his blood, made him whimper and cower like a camp cur. He was grinning wide when he strode into the circle of lodges, feeling tall and manly, victorious for the first time in his life.

Inside his lodge, in the cool, he began to shake for no reason at all. He wondered if Red Tracks would come after him with a club and beat him for revenge. He jumped at every sound until his mother looked at him oddly.

"There is blood on your hands," she said softly.

"Ah. I cut myself."

He was not lying. He looked at his knuckles and they were scraped but the blood was not his own. His mother snorted and shooed him from the lodge.

"You come back when you do not jump and make me jump," she said. "Bear Heart will want you to go with him to see Old Lodge when the sun goes to sleep."

Eats-Meat scooted from the lodge, ran to the river. He jumped in and swam until he was calm. He saw no more of Red Tracks that day and his heart was full. He wanted to tell the other boys what he had done, but after he thought of it for a time, it felt better to keep this good secret to himself. He had bested Red Tracks, but no one had seen this thing and Red Tracks, he was sure, would not speak with a straight tongue, but out of the side of his mouth. He dove under the waters and opened his eyes. In the murky light he thought he saw another world and it was his own world and nothing could hurt him there. The waters were full of shimmering wonders and bright glitters that changed colors as they swirled in the churn of his body. He emerged from beneath the water, swam lazily to the bank, flung himself on the shore. He looked up at the blue sky for a long time, felt the sun burn strength back into his muscles.

It was the best day of his life.

CHAPTER FOUR

As the sun went to sleep, making the land and the mountains gray, the warriors began to leave their lodges, walk toward Old Lodge's *tipi*. Eats-Meat went with his father, Bear Heart. There was a hush to the camp and even the dogs were quiet as the processions converged on the medicine lodge where Old Lodge would sing and call in the spirits.

Old Lodge stood there in front of his dwelling as the light leaked out of the sky and fell beyond the mountains. He held his arms out from his sides, the palms upward, and lifted his head to the darkening sky. His gray hair was twined in a single braid, his torso naked. His breechclout hung over his sash, dangled between his legs. His moccasins were planted far apart. He opened his mouth, began to chant.

O hear me spirits, open your ears.
I call you. I am Old Lodge. Suh-tai hetan.
I am Suh-tai man. Tell me what you see.
I listen. Tell me. Tell me. Make me see.

He sang these words over and over and he made the signs with his hands flying like nightbirds and then he closed his mouth tight and his body went rigid. Old Lodge stood there like a stone pillar, unmoving, and the people were very quiet. Even the dogs and the children made no sound while the spirits spoke to Old

Lodge, whispered their secrets in his open ears, whispered to him in silent tongues so that only his heart could hear their words.

When Old Lodge was finished listening to the spirits, he told everyone what he had heard.

"You who go to the Crow on foot will catch many horses. These will be fine horses, but there is one that has hair white as the moon and a tail with the hair chopped short. This horse you will bring to me. No one will know who has the horse in his bunch until the next sun wakes up. But this man must say, 'This one is your horse, Old Lodge,' and he must bring it back to me. You who catch this horse will want to keep it, but if you do, the spirits have told me they will be very angry because they want me to have this horse. If you promise that this white horse will be given to me when you return you will come back safely. No enemy will harm you or catch you."

The men who were going after the Crow horses all grunted in agreement. Old Lodge turned and went inside his tipi and closed the flap. The people began to walk back to their lodges. Eats-Meat-Quickly did not understand the meaning of Old Lodge's words. He asked his father, when they were alone, why the spirits had given the white horse to Old Lodge.

"I do not know this," said Bear Heart. "But this is a good thing. If the man who catches the white horse makes the promise to give it to Old Lodge, then the Crow cannot catch us. We will come back with many horses."

"Will you give up the white horse if you catch it?"

"Yes. It must be a spirit horse and it would be bad to

keep it when the spirits have said that it belongs to Old Lodge."

Eats-Meat thought that he understood what his father was saying, but he could hardly sleep all night, thinking of the bobbed-tail horse with a hide like the full shining moon.

The men and boys painted for war, and gathered up the things they would take on the journey. The sun woke up when they were ready, lapping up all the shadows on the prairie, licking off the dew from the grasses, smoothing the wrinkles out of the mountains.

Eats-Meat was sure that his mother, Corn Woman, could hear his heart thumping against his ribs, so he made a lot of noise as he checked his arrows, the flint points, the fletching, the straightness of the shafts. He knocked over an iron kettle, bonked his head on a lodgepole, rattled the arrows in his quiver until she looked up from the fire and fixed him with a look.

"You will wake the spirits," she said.

Bear Heart grunted as he smeared the last of the yellow ocher on his chest.

"Come," he said, "you must get the sacred arrows from Old Lodge."

Eats-Meat snatched up his lance. The hawk feathers tied below the chipped flint blade fluttered, twirled on thin, greasy sinew.

Corn Woman handed her men the little buckskin bags of dried meat and berries that had been pounded into a ball. Her fingers trembled as they flickered over her son's body like mindless starlings flapping at the smokehole of a tipi.

"Catch many horses," she muttered to Bear Heart, as

he ducked through the tentflap. To her son, she said nothing, but her eyes filled with the dew of morning and she shrank back into the shadows of the lodge, her lips drawn tight to her teeth.

Eats-Meat's moccasins whispered against the earth as he followed his father to the gathering at Old Lodge's tipi. He gripped his bow and quiver tight so that they did not make noise, but he still heard his blood pound hard in his ears, felt his heart like a small thunder in his chest.

Spotted Dog was there and Lightning Lance, Rope Earrings, too, speaking to Old Lodge, and Red Tracks glowered as he stood next to his father, his face painted fierce, a big flint knife jutting from its double-thick sheath, the beadwork fine as any Eats-Meat had seen. And the air was thick with the smell of dried meat and berries, the tang of warpaint, the musk of animal-skin clothing. Eats-Meat stayed close to Bear Heart, but Spotted Dog tugged at his elbow, drew him away to whisper excitedly in his ear.

"My belly is full of mosquitoes," the boy said.

"Mine too. Did you see the buffalo hat?"

"There," he pointed and Eats-Meat saw it on the wardrum, lying on a swatch of squared-off buffalo robe. He saw the medicine arrows, too, on another drumhead, each one laid out on an elkskin hide with the sacred markings, the fringes long and delicate, the thongs loose so all could see that the arrowtips were shiny, without blood. The things looked magic to Eats-Meat. He could almost feel their power burning into him, scorching his face, searing his eyes. He looked away and drew in a deep breath because his stomach

swirled with a kind of dread that had no word for it, no
name.

When the warriors were all gathered there by the
medicine lodge, Old Lodge cleared his throat of the
dust that comes in the night and spoke in brisk words to
the assemblage. He held before him the hooped lance
that was his proudest possession.

"I lend this *hohk tsim* to Rope Earrings," he said, "so
that he can lead you to the Crow, bring back many
horses." He handed the lance with the hoop on it to
Rope Earrings. "Guard it well. Do not let it be captured. If it is taken from you by any man, harm will
come to us."

"I will do this," promised Rope Earrings, who took
the lance, stepped back. The warriors murmured their
approval at this deed. Another brave, this one known
for his pride, looked at Rope Earrings with envy. This
one was called Flying Deer and there were many scars
on his chest from the sundance.

"Now, I will do the ceremony that will protect you
and confuse the enemy," said Old Lodge.

A hush fell over the group of painted men and boys,
as Old Lodge stepped to the wardrums where the buffalo hat and the sacred arrows were displayed.

Eats-Meat looked at the sacred objects again. They
seemed to pulse with life, with a power he could almost
feel in his bones. The little hairs on his arms stood up,
bristled with a sudden chill.

The arrows were beautiful, four in number, with the
stone points of ancient days. The sacred hat was a thick
bonnet made from the skin of the buffalo cow's head.
The horns were shaved down, polished to a high sheen

with sandstone, flattened and painted with sacred colors and designs.

"These medicine arrows," intoned Old Lodge, "were sent by the Great Power to give us, his people, health, long life, and plenty of meat in the times when we do not fight. These gifts protect us. They give our people strength. They give us victory over our enemies in war. The medicine arrows were brought to the Tsis-tsis-tas by Sweet Medicine. The buffalo hat was given to the Suh-tai by Standing on the Ground.

"My father gave me these sacred things, and his father gave them to him. They are very old, and they have been restored many times, with new sinew wrapped around the stone points, new feathers on the shafts. These things have been done when there was trouble, or to make apology for bad things done.

"These two boys here, Spotted Dog and Eats-Meat-Quickly, have been chosen to carry the sacred arrows and the buffalo hat into battle. I ask the spirits to guard them and protect them from harm."

Old Lodge stepped back to the drumhead where the arrows were displayed and picked up a root that was always tied up with the arrows. He bit off a piece of it, chewed it for a long time until it was shredded fine. He blew pieces of the root to the four points of the compass and finally turned in the direction where the scouts had spotted the Crow. He blew the remaining bits of root toward the enemy, spitting the shreds from his mouth in a vigorous spray.

"Blind the Crow," he chanted to the spirits. "Confuse them. Make them run around in circles. Put the fear of the rabbit in their hearts."

Old Lodge then picked up the arrows and began to dance. The mass of braves around him backed away to give him room. An opening parted in the semicircle of painted men, allowing the arrow-keeper to dance through. Old Lodge pointed the arrows toward the enemy camp and thrust them in time to his dancing feet. He kept moving in the direction of the Crow camp and the warriors all formed a line behind him.

Eats-Meat stood in line like the others, behind his father. Each man danced the same steps as Old Lodge and Eats-Meat followed their lead. He shook his lance when Old Lodge shook the arrows, pointed it at the enemy when the arrow-keeper did. The dance was slow, methodical, like a man stalking the enemy, and Old Lodge thrust the arrows four times and the lances and axes were thrust four times also.

Old Lodge thrust the arrows for a fifth time, toward the ground. Then he stood up straight and stiff, began to sing the songs to the spirits.

> *Make the arrows fly true.*
> *Make them strike the enemy.*
> *Make the lances of our people*
> *draw the blood of the Crow.*

He sang, and Eats-Meat stood transfixed, his blood singing in his veins, his muscles quivering, his hand tight around his lance. He listened to the warsongs, tried to fix the words in his mind so that he would remember them later if they had to fight the Crow. But the words slipped through his mind like creek water over mossy stone, and yet they dug into his heart, fired his blood. He saw and felt the immense power of the songs in the gravel-throated chant of Old Lodge and he knew the medicine of the arrows he would carry was strong. He had no fear in his heart.

Abruptly, the singing stopped.

Eats-Meat, still dazed by the ceremony, heard his name being called.

His father nudged him out of the line of men, pushed him gently toward Old Lodge.

"Come," said the arrow-keeper, "I will wrap the arrows, give them to you."

Old Lodge and the boy walked back to the drums. Slowly, he wrapped the sacred arrows into the bundle with the roots, lashed them tight to Eats-Meat's lance. He called Spotted Dog out of the line and told him to pick up the sacred buffalo hat. Spotted Dog put the hat on his head, tied it under his chin with the two pieces of rawhide string.

"Go," said Old Lodge, and pointed in the direction of the enemy.

Eats-Meat and Spotted Dog turned and strode from the camp on foot. Behind them, the warriors came, rattling their lances, singing their private war songs.

The two boys did not look back.

Bear Heart's son walked lightfooted as the sun struck them in their faces. They would go to the enemy on foot because they would steal horses and ride back fast as the wind that blew through the mountains.

Flying Deer walked behind Rope Earrings, his face drawn up into a scowl under his warpaint. Bear Heart saw that the warrior was not singing, saw that his face was bad, but he said nothing. Instead, he strode up to walk beside Rope Earrings.

"When we find the Crow," he said softly, "let me watch your back if there is fighting."

Rope Earrings broke off his song, turned his head slightly.

"I know the man you speak of, Bear Heart," he said. "He has a bad heart this day."

Flying Deer made a choking sound in his throat, and his eyes turned fierce as a cougar's. He heard the whispering between Bear Heart and Rope Earrings. But he did not hear the words. Yet he knew what they were saying, even so, and his jealousy rose up in his chest and smothered him like the smoke from wet firewood.

There were two dozen men and boys on the war party, that day, walking into the sun as it rose, walking toward the little stream that runs into the Yellowstone. In a far meadow, a bull elk bugled, and the sound lingered in the air for a long time as the men stopped singing and began saving their breaths for the march.

CHAPTER FIVE

Flying Deer was a proud man, a Crooked Lance Soldier, one of the few of that society with Old Lodge's camp. It was said that he was very brave, but in a fight with the Crow a few years before, when the Crooked Lances were ambushed, he was the only one to survive. He was thought dead by the Crow since his scalp was taken, but he did not die and his hair grew back because the scalping knife had not sheared him to the skullbone.

He was asleep for many days after he was found, and when he woke up, he did not seem to be much in the world. He muttered to himself and often sat for hours staring into the empty sky or at the coals of a fire. The people left him alone, and one day he painted himself, took his lance and his bow, rode off on his pony. People spoke to him and asked him where he was going, but he did not answer. He was gone for three days and when he returned, he had five Crow scalps hanging from his lance. He did not dance the victory dance, then, nor did he describe what he had done at the tribe's annual gatherings. But he was the fiercest man at the sundances and he sank the skewers in deep. When he fainted, he talked strangely and people avoided him because they thought he was possessed of spirits.

He went away once again, but this time he did not

bring back Crow scalps. Instead, he brought with him a fine shield, one that many envied because it was made of tough bullhide and strong enough to stop an arrow or turn a ball from the white man's shooting sticks that were smooth inside the hollow part.

Flying Deer carried this shield now, on his left arm, and its emblems proclaimed it sacred to the thunder and to the lightning. It was adorned with the feathers of the eagle and so gave its owner the swiftness and courage of that bird. But, most awesome of all, painted in the center of the shield was a snarling bear standing on its hind legs, and attached to the bottom and top of the shield, their points aimed outward, were the claws of a bear. And no one knew where Flying Deer got the claws, but they were fresh claws when he came back to camp with the shield, and they were still bloody from being yanked from living flesh.

After he came back with the thunderbear shield, Flying Deer no longer smoked in his lodge, and no one asked him how he had gotten the shield nor questioned his right to carry it, because it also bore the dream markings of the Crooked Lances and this was a society held in much esteem by the people. When he wore the shield into battle, as now, people did not look on him as ordinary, because they believed his shield had much power and they believed that the bear and the eagle had spoken to Flying Deer and told him how to make such a fine and beautiful shield.

"I will scout ahead," Flying Deer told Rope Earrings, even though the leader had not spoken to Flying Deer. They had come many strides down the little creek that runs into the Yellowstone and the sun was falling toward its sleeping place, but still high.

"The Crow are two suns," said Rope Earrings, surprised that Flying Deer would speak to him like that. But, he looked at the shield and felt its power, so he did not show anger.

"I will see if there are Crow where we go."

"Do not alarm them if you see any. You come and tell us where they are."

Flying Deer grunted and then loped off ahead of them, his braids flopping on his sweat-sleeked back. He passed the two boys, Spotted Dog and Eats-Meat, who, startled, danced to one side and then looked back at Rope Earrings.

"I do not know why he does this," said Bear Heart to Rope Earrings. "This is a bad thing."

"He hates the Crow."

"We go to steal, not to do battle."

"With the Crow, sometimes the two sticks cross."

Rope Earrings took the head of the column then, ordered the others to fan out, stay to the trees along the little creek. The two boys with the medicine arrows and buffalo hat frowned when they were sent back to the rear where they could be watched by the older warriors.

But Eats-Meat felt the excitement now, and he was choking with the wish to ask his father where Flying Deer had gone running. He watched the men-warriors slink through the trees, Whistling Elk and Bear Above, Wolf Face, Thin Face, Big Nose, Wolf Road, and he saw Red Tracks ranging ahead of him, flitting through the trees like a brown shadow.

Rope Earrings sent trackers out and the war party settled into a steady walk. The men ate from their food pouches without stopping, and drank little water. At one place, they saw the tracks of buffalo, and at another, antelope spoor. The smell of game was strong, stronger than the scent of balsam and pine, fir and cedar. Eats-Meat began to feel the tendons in his legs turning sore, but after a while they loosened up and he did not hurt anymore.

Rope Earrings made the signs with his hands and the band gathered together at a wide, grassy spot where the creek made a bend. The sun was trying to hide in the mountains before it went to sleep and there were long shadows on the ground. The warrior held them to silence for a long time, as he put his ear to the ground. Others did the same, and some put their hands to their ears so that they could hear far-off sounds. A few moments later, Eats-Meat heard a sound of leaves rubbing together and then he saw Flying Deer emerge from the shadows of an alder thicket.

Rope Earrings stood up, waited for Flying Deer to approach. The scout passed close to Eats-Meat and Spotted Dog. Gone was his lance and shield. His body was streaming sweat, his warpaint streaked, smeared, clots of dirt rubbed into the skin on his face and legs. His eyes burned with a fierce light.

The two boys followed Flying Deer, walking several paces behind until he met Rope Earrings in the center of the clearing.

"The Crow make camp below big creek," said Flying Deer. "Many horses. Many braves."

"Where is your lance and your shield?"

Flying Deer turned his face away in shame.

"Did they catch you?"

Flying Deer did not answer.

Rope Earrings spoke to all of them.

"The Crow have moved their camp. They are close to us, but we are ready. They cannot see us. We will go where they are. We will hide in the creek bottom until the sun goes to sleep. Do not eat much. Rest and think about this thing we will do. Flying Deer has seen the Crow and now he knows they have many horses for us."

Eats-Meat knew that Rope Earrings did not want to shame Flying Deer and as he listened to the warrior's words, his stomach began to quiver. He was ready to go to the Crow and catch their horses. He looked at Spotted Dog, who smiled at him with a sickly grin. Spotted Dog was trembling all over and his face showed that the blood had drained away into his neck.

The men talked in low tones as they prepared to go to the Crow camp. They checked their lances and bows, their knives and arrows. Some chewed on dried meat. Eats-Meat heard a boy give up his food in the bushes and he felt shame for him. He did not eat because his belly was churned up like a tidepool in a fast-running stream, quivering like a fish caught with the hands.

Rope Earrings sent two of the best scouts downriver, Buffalo Horn and Walking Eagle. Flying Deer made sign with his hands to show them where the Crows had made camp, and then he turned his face away from them, sulked alone at the edge of the alder thicket. The war party began a silent walk along the little creek, following Rope Earrings and Bear Heart. There would be no thunder of pony hooves to give them away, but all knew that there was danger because one of the Crow had fought Flying Deer and had taken away his lance and shield.

The sun seemed to hang in the sky as if caught on one of the distant peaks, pulsing with orange fire, blinding Eats-Meat when he looked at it. He wondered if it would not go to sleep, but just stay there forever. He wished it would go to sleep so the Crow could not see them as they crept along the creek toward their camp.

Scouts came and went like ghostly shapes in the trees, made sign to Rope Earrings, then disappeared again. Eats-Meat felt the excitement build inside him until he jumped at every faint sound. He listened to the soft footpads of those stalking men around him, heard the rustle of tanned deerhide against tree branches, the rattle of an overturned stone, the wheeze-breath of a warrior as he passed him in a silent lope. His ears seemed to open up like the deer's so that he could hear sounds more sharply and he tried to be still himself, make no noise that would alert the enemy.

The sun dropped off the mountains and smeared the sky with its colored dust and soon even that faded away into shadow spoor and then even those last traces of the sun's journey were gone, swallowed up by the darkness. Rope Earrings waited for them, stopped the men, signed them to lie in the streambed and rest. Eats-Meat hunkered low against the bank, breathing hard, hating the noise he made like a wind sniffing the tipi, pulling at the doorflap. As his breathing steadied, he heard the other sounds, the ones that came from far away and had no direction, at first. He heard the distant whicker of a pony, the yap-yap-yap of a cur. Voices. The short wail of a child that was quickly silenced.

He looked at the others, saw them grow dim, waver like leaf shadows in water, lose their shape until they were just dark blotches tucked inside light clothing without form or substance. He felt the beginnings of fear stir in him, and he began to imagine that he was all alone because it was so quiet and no one spoke. He had to strain to hear his own breathing now, because he was almost not breathing and the dark was suffocating him with its smothering buffalo blanket.

He did not see time as anything but emptiness, as the slight, unseen movement of stars, as things that happened between empty places in his heart. He looked at the stars and saw no movement, and he looked away, at the ground, then back again and there was still no movement, so it seemed as if everything in the world had just stopped while they were waiting and he closed his eyes and heard the pounding of his heart, very faint and like the wary tread of a deer through the forest. He was not sure that this was his heart sounding in his ears and thought that the Crow were sneaking up on them, ready to brain them with warclubs. He could almost hear them shouting in that place behind his eyes where he saw his thoughts. Then, he gulped for air and opened his eyes and saw only the stolid shapes in the same places, the darker shadows growing out of tanned hides that had dulled under the glaze of night.

A shadow moved down the streambed and bent at each other shadow and he saw the man's hand move with sign, like a silent bat. A stone creaked and a man stood against the black skyline, then another man and another, until they were all moving, and Eats-Meat was among them, shivering with fear, choked with the excitement that rattled his mind like seeds in a medicine man's antelope scrotum.

The Cheyenne slid over the bank of the dry creek, ran, crouching, toward the Crow camp. Out of the darkness, Bear Heart appeared, whispered into Eats-Meat's ear.

"You must point the arrows, do the dance. Make no sound."

Confused, the boy hesitated, then remembered Old Lodge and the war dance with the medicine arrows. Eats-Meat grasped the lance, pointed it in the direction of the Crow camp and began to imitate the dance he had seen. He bobbed and wriggled in the darkness as the shadow shapes slipped by him, fanned out. He smelled the scent of the horses, smelled their droppings on the night air.

The dance calmed him, but the lance was awkward, off-centered by the bundle of arrows. He stumbled and, although he made no noise, his heart jumped in his chest and his face flushed with blood.

Closer and closer, the Cheyenne warriors crept, until Eats-Meat saw the massed hulk of the pony herd. He heard a sound, froze in his dance and saw a Crow brave locked in a deathgrip by a Cheyenne. There was another crunch, as a flint knife struck bone and gristle. The Crow made a grunt sound like passing wind and the Cheyenne seemed to caress him like a spider embraces a fly. The Crow gave up his spirit quick. The Cheyenne stepped away, leaving the Crow laid out on the ground like a man asleep.

Eats-Meat did not know what to do. He saw his brothers disappear into the herd like fish diving through clusters of minnows and then ponies started moving, fanning out, strings of them and bunches, until the earth itself seemed to be breaking up, exploding in silent chunks.

A Crow shouted the alarm, and then the Cheyenne began to shout insults and curses and scream at the ponies. Eats-Meat heard the whisper of an arrow in flight. The shaft struck a rock and he saw sparks fly off from the flint in a miniature shower.

"Get yourself a pony, quick!" Eats-Meat turned, saw Spotted Dog wrestling a pinto, trying to jump on its back. The fear rose up in Eats-Meat again, but it mingled with a strange feeling of excitement, a drenching exhilaration. Then, Spotted Dog scrambled atop the pony's back and let out a youthful whoop as he grabbed its mane, clapped moccasins into its flanks.

Eats-Meat ran toward the herd. Ponies whinnied in terror, milled, trampled the ground. He ran toward a bunch, panting with excitement. He grabbed a pony's tail, pulled hard. The pony backed up, lifted its hind quarters into the air and kicked with both legs. Eats-Meat ducked under and, still holding the tail, circled it. He jabbed the animal with the butt of his lance, pushed it sideways. He ran to its head, grabbed a handful of mane. His bow slapped against him as he threw himself on the animal's back. He struggled to stay on the heaving, slippery hide, dug his heels into the flanks.

Eats-Meat held on, then turned the pony out of the packed bunch. He jabbed with his lance, yanked at the mane and the pony responded to its new master.

"Aiiieeeeyaaaaaa!" screeched Eats-Meat as the pony gathered speed, broke away from the swirling mass of animals, headed for open ground. All around him, horses were moving, and he saw his brothers herding bunches of them toward the creek. Some of the Cheyenne had already put their rope halters on the stolen mounts they rode and he wished he had done the same. But he followed the strings of ponies and no longer had to use the lance. He placed it crosswise in front of him, the medicine arrows safe in their bundle which nudged against his lap.

The Crow camp burst alive. Eats-Meat saw men running, heard them yelling, and then the sounds faded as he rode through dust, tasted grit between his teeth, twitched his nose before he sneezed.

Pony hooves made thunders on the earth and jubilant cries of Cheyenne pierced the night, floated through the trees like ghost voices, fading and echoing, thrilling him as he followed blindly, racing fast and ducking the swaying branches that emerged out of the dust and darkness like grasping hands.

The air washed him, cooled his sweat, traced furrows through his hair. He touched the bundle of medicine arrows and felt only empty hide. His hand punched, his fingers groped for the sacred arrows, but they were not there. He pulled on the pony's mane, tried to stop it, but the animal bucked and then charged ahead, chasing after the other ponies, rushing through the dust and the dark with its empty head of stone. Eats-Meat screamed at the dumb animal to stop, but it kept going, faster and faster, and the boy cursed it, cried out in helpless rage until the tears came and the hurt squeezed his throat until he had no voice anymore. He sank back on his buttocks and felt the empty bundle once again, hoping he had only dreamed it all, hoping that the spirits had only played a trick on him.

But the arrows, sacred to his people, were gone, lost somewhere in the darkness, back there where the Crow would find them and destroy them.

Eats-Meat did not know the pony had stopped running. In his heart, the boy was still riding fast, trying to escape his own shame, the terrible dejection that gripped him like the eagle's talons.

The pony blew twin plumes of steam through its nostrils as it halted, shook like a wet dog. Eats-Meat saw that the other ponies had stopped, too, and he saw men on horseback all around him. He heard the men grunt with pleasure and pant words of their victory.

Eats-Meat heard these things and saw the others, but he had never been more alone in his life. Inside, he was empty as a cornhusk, and his spirit sad as the autumn earth filling up with the skeletons of dry dead leaves.

CHAPTER SIX

Eats-Meat-Quickly choked back a sob, a cry of anguish that rose up in his throat from some deep place of hurt inside him. He blinked back the stinging tears and gulped in air, holding it in his lungs until he felt a calm settle in the swirl of fear-thoughts raging through his mind. He turned the pony, his heart a throb of thunder in his chest, and rode back in the direction from which he had come.

No one must know that he lost the sacred arrows. He must find them, put them back in the bundle. But where were they? When had he lost them? He did not know, but they were back there, somewhere, perhaps trampled by the ponies, perhaps just lying on the ground in the darkness.

He tried to remember the path he had taken, looked at the pitch earth and felt his heart sink like a falling eagle. It was so dark he did not know if he could find the arrows, and what if the slash of pony hooves had broken them, scattered them like dead leaves? He would never find them and the Cheyenne medicine would turn bad. He licked dry lips, felt the taste of brackish saliva in his mouth as if he had drunk from a stagnant pool.

He heard someone shout his name, and his spine stiffened as he jerked upright on the pony's back.

"Eats-Meat, where do you go? Come back." Bear

Heart called to him and the boy did not turn, but muttered something that he knew could not be heard.

Ponies streamed by him, whipped on by faceless braves of his own tribe. He guided the pony with his knees, turned the animal away from the flood of Crow ponies, but heard his name called again.

"Why are you running away?" Red Tracks shouted from behind Eats-Meat. The older boy caught up, rode alongside Eats-Meat.

"Go away."

Red Tracks did not go away. He stayed by Eats-Meat, guiding his pony with the horsehair halter, taunting the younger boy.

"You are going the wrong way."

"Leave me. Go back," pleaded Eats-Meat.

"You are up to something bad. Your father is calling you and you do not answer."

"I—I forgot something."

Red Tracks rode in close, raked a hand across the empty bundle. Eats-Meat raised his lance to strike him. He wanted to kill Red Tracks at that moment. He wanted to knock him from his pony, drive him into the ground, mash him to pulp like the berries crushed into pemmican meat.

"You did not steal but one pony," taunted Red Tracks. "I captured five and am going back for more."

"I am going to steal many ponies," boasted Eats-Meat.

As soon as he had said it, Eats-Meat knew that he must do what he said he would do. It was exciting to steal one pony, but he must steal more. First, though, he must find the sacred medicine arrows.

A figure on horseback loomed out of the darkness, his silhouette cloaked in shadow.

Thunder Wind, the father of Red Tracks, drove a dozen horses past them, then hauled his horse to a halt by a tug on the reins of the horsehair halter.

"You go back for more ponies?"

"Yes, my father," said Red Tracks.

"There are many Crow running around like crazy. They have bows and they are shooting. Do not go close to the camp."

"This one has lost the sacred arrows," said Thunder Wind's son.

Eats-Meat felt his face grow hot as if a firewind blew against it. He backed his pony away, rode toward the Crow camp, shamed. Behind him, he heard the two men laughing at him.

Ponies milled everywhere, streaked by him as he tried to get his bearings. He rode to the place where he had caught the pony and leaned over to look at the ground. He rode in wide circles, then backtracked, trying to remember everything he had done after that. He rode to the creek, saw a shaft jutting from between stones. He leaped from the pony, letting it run away. He jerked the arrow free, peered at it intently in the darkness.

It was one of the medicine arrows. He smelled its wooden shaft, touched its point in fear. A jubilant cry rose up in his throat, but he choked it back, began to scramble along the creek bed looking for the other arrows. Grasping his lance and the found arrow in one hand, he crabbed over the rocks, feeling with the fingers of his left hand, groping in the crevices. His heart beat fast in his chest and his stomach muscles knotted, quivered.

Around him, he heard the thunder of ponies, the shouts of Crow and Cheyenne braves, the whistle of arrows, the shrill keening of women in the camp. He tried to shut out the noises, clambered up and down the banks of the creekbed, his heart thumping thumping like running feet in his chest, the blood thrum strong in his pulsing temples.

A few steps farther on, he found two more arrows. One lay in the center of the streambed, the other was halfway up the bank. That was the direction he had ridden, and now his heart soared like a hawk as he scrambled up the bank and headed toward the trees. His eyes seemed to burn in their sockets as he sought the remaining arrow in the shadows. A pair of ponies broke from the cover of the trees and cleared the creekbed where it narrowed. The sound made his heart jump, but he quelled the fear and searched all around as he trod forward, following the path he had taken earlier.

The fourth arrow leaned against a tree where it had fallen. Eats-Meat cried out in exultation, dashed for the arrow. As he stretched out his hand to grab it up, a figure stepped from behind a tree a dozen paces away. The boy froze in his tracks for several heartbeats, then reached for the arrow. He grasped it tightly as the shadowy figure strode toward him.

"So, you found them all," said Red Tracks.

Eats-Meat backed away, clutching the arrows and his lance.

"Stay away from me," he said.

"Give me those arrows. You are not the one to carry them any longer."

"No."

Eats-Meat turned and ran just as Red Tracks broke into a charge. He heard the older boy calling for him to stop, but he kept running, across the creek and back toward the dark cloud of milling ponies.

The dark became ominous with shadows, with ponies turning into the shapes of men, flashing by him from all directions. He reached out a feeble hand to grab a mane and a pony twisted away from him, its snorting nostrils spraying his face with wet, hot steam.

He choked on the dust, squeezed his eyes to slits as the animals swirled around him like the shadows of forgotten ancestors and he plunged toward a pony caught in the stampede; the animal halted, confused, stopped in midflight, staggering in circles.

Eats-Meat grabbed the pony's tail, digging his fingers into the strands of hair, grasping the fleshy stump and holding on as the animal tried to bolt away. The pony bucked and tried to gallop free, but other horses blocked its way. The Cheyenne youth tightened his hold, dug in the heels of his moccasins.

The pony jerked the boy off his feet, dragged him through the pack of milling animals. Eats-Meat hung on, felt the pain shoot through his wrist, up his arm. His muscles rippled as the tendons tautened under the strain. The pony broke free of the herd, galloped onto the dark plain. Dust hung in the air like smoke and scratched at Eats-Meat's eyes. Still, he hung on, and soon he felt the pony tiring. The animal slowed, tried to kick at him. Eats-Meat jerked hard on the tail, regained his footing. He began to run with the horse, catch his second wind.

Finally, the pony, its breath wheezing in its chest, halted. It tossed its mane and eyed the attachment on its tail, snorted, stamped a hoof. Eats-Meat clutched his weapons, the sacred arrows, tucked them under his left armpit. Pain scorched his lungs as he gulped air. Gradually, he relaxed his grip on the pony's tail, moving his hand up over its rump very slowly. He sidled around the left flank of the animal, spoke to it in gasping, soothing tones.

"Be quiet. Let me ride you, pony."

The pony whickered, as Eats-Meat touched its mane, gathered the hair in his fist. He waited until his breathing returned to normal, then took another hitch in the mane, swung atop the pony's back. He sat there for several moments, gripping the mane. Then, he touched moccasined heels to the animal's flanks, twisted the clump of mane. The pony stepped out, turned in the direction Eats-Meat pulled on its mane.

The boy chuckled in satisfaction, swelled his chest with a deep, gulping breath. He looked around him, listened to the shouts of men, the thunder of pony hooves, as more and more captured animals galloped away from the Crow camp.

He heard screams of men in agony, heard the terrible Crow curses, the brash oaths of angered Cheyenne braves, and the night seemed to darken as his heart pumped hard with a nameless fear. He could not fight, for he would have to drop the sacred bundle of arrows. He rode the pony like a cripple, afraid it would run out from under him, or rear up and slide him off its back.

He jabbered to the pony with the summoned words of a braggart, words that floated false to his ears.

"You are my pony," he said. "I am a strong Cheyenne brave. You will go where I tell you, Crow pony, or I will beat you with a stick."

His throat went dry as the pony threaded its way through the driven pack, jostling the rider at every twist and turn. Eats-Meat hunched over, clamping his legs tight against the animal's flanks.

He knew the way to the meeting place now and he guided the pony toward the creek.

Eats-Meat saw a man ride by him, driving five horses. He recognized him by the song he was singing. It was Flying Deer. Then, he saw the white pony and his heart leaped up into his throat. At first he thought it was a ghost-pony, a spirit horse, because it was shining like the moon and Eats-Meat could not hear its hooves strike the ground because his ears were plugged up with the pounding of his own blood.

"I have caught the white pony," shouted Flying Deer. "Look, you all, I have caught the white pony."

Then they were at the meeting place and Eats-Meat's heart fluttered with joy that he had returned and had the sacred arrows with him. He looked at all the men on foot, saw them tying ropes to their captured ponies, leading them to private, separate places, and he saw his father, Bear Heart, away from the others, putting rope to a big spotted pony.

"Look, my father," he said. "I have caught a fine pony."

"Yes, I have some rope for you."

The young man slid from his pony's back, held tight

to its mane. He breathed hard, but felt his heart soar. Bear Heart handed him a length of rope and he made a circle with it, knotted it around his pony's neck. He tied the pony to a small tree and stood by it, panting as more ponies came into the camp and the men sang their boasting songs.

"I saw the white pony," said Eats-Meat.

"What do you say?" asked his father.

"Flying Deer caught the white pony. I saw it. It was as Old Lodge said it would be. A fine white pony, white as the winter moon."

He heard his father draw in a breath, but he could not see Bear Heart's face. The older man said nothing.

"That is good, is it not? Father? Now the Crow cannot catch us. Our medicine is strong. I still have the medicine arrows. I did not . . . did not lose them."

There was no answer.

"Father?"

Bear Heart tightened a knot, grunted. He tied the loose end of the rope to the fork of a tree, walked over to his son.

"Spotted Dog is dead," he said. "The buffalo hat is gone."

Eats-Meat felt a suffocating hand tighten around his windpipe as his throat constricted. His mouth went dry and he felt giddy.

"How do you know?"

"Rope Earrings brought the boy back. Two Crow struck him twice apiece and another drove a lance through his stomach. The Crow took the medicine hat and ran off before anyone could catch them and kill them."

Eats-Meat choked off the sob that wrenched his throat, gulped in air. Mist streaked his eyes and his father's face swam like a reflection in a stream.

"No," he gasped.

He felt his father's hand slapping him on the muscle of his shoulder. It was like the swipe of a paw, did not hurt, but jarred him. He looked up, saw the dark shadow of Bear Heart's face, like a mask without eyes or expression and he knew that it was true. Spotted Dog was dead and the medicine hat gone, stolen by the Crow.

"What about the white pony?" he asked in desperation.

"I do not know. If Flying Deer gives it up, maybe the Crow will not catch us. Do not lose the medicine arrows. That would finish us all."

"No," said the boy, his lips quivering.

He wanted to tell his father what had happened, but Bear Heart turned away from him, stalked through the filling-up camp and Eats-Meat was alone, fighting down the grief for his friend, quaking with fear over the loss of the medicine hat.

He wondered now if Spotted Dog had been killed while the arrows were lost.

Yes, this must be so.

He blamed himself for his friend's death, the loss of the buffalo hat.

"Bear Heart, my father," he shouted feebly. "Wait. I must tell you a thing."

He pushed away from the tree, started to run after Bear Heart, but a shadow loomed beside him and a strong hand gripped his arm just above the elbow.

"Young man. Let me see the arrows."

The voice belonged to Rope Earrings.

"Why? I have them."

"Open the bundle."

Eats-Meat, with trembling fingers, opened the hide bundle. The arrows rattled like stones rolled down a hill. The warrior picked up each arrow in turn.

"*Wougghh,*" he grunted. "This one is broken."

"No," gasped Eats-Meat.

Rope Earrings held up the arrow. It was in two pieces. Even in the dark, Eats-Meat could see it. His earlobes burned as if someone had touched fire to them.

"This is bad. This is the death of little Spotted Dog and the stealing of the medicine hat."

"I—I did not break the arrow," blurted Eats-Meat and he knew it was true.

"No. But the arrow is broken, and the buffalo hat gone, young man. Do not tell any man. It would not be good for the others to know this. Not even Bear Heart. Do you hear my words?"

Eats-Meat grunted in reply.

Rope Earrings put the broken arrow back in the bundle, folded it up tight. He tied it secure to Eats-Meat's lance and strode away a few yards. He turned and the boy could see that his shoulders were shaking. The feathers in his hair shook, too.

"Do not blame yourself for these things, young man. You have done well. You got the arrows back and we can ask Old Lodge to make new ones for us."

Eats-Meat's heart turned in his chest, sank like a stone. So, Rope Earrings knew he had lost the arrows.

But, they were not broken. Not when he found them. How? How, then, had this thing happened?

He wanted to ask Rope Earrings, someone, but the warrior padded away in silence.

Eats-Meat sagged to the ground, clutching his lance, the sacred bundle of medicine arrows.

The night seemed to blacken close around him again, like a cold blanket, smothering him. But he did not care if he could not breathe. He slumped to the ground, cuddled the arrows to his breast, and let the sobs flood from his throat and shake him as the mountain shook the earth when pieces of it broke off and rumbled downward in a roar of rocks and broken trees.

CHAPTER SEVEN

The Cheyennes began driving the ponies away from the meeting place long before dawn. Rope Earrings led the way, and Bear Heart brought up the rear to make sure that there were no stragglers. Eats-Meat-Quickly rode at his father's side, afraid of becoming lost as the column stretched out. The ponies were ghostly shapes streaming on all sides of him and his own mount finally settled into a gait that matched the other horses.

The boy lost all sense of direction. The land looked different in the dark and he saw no signs or shapes of any earth thing that he knew. Hours later, he was rubbing his eyes and yawning as the excitement inside him began to ebb. When the sun woke up, he began to lose his sleepiness. The faces of men riding by him began to take on features and the sky was the color of skinned salmon for a long time.

Rope Earrings called a halt when the sun was full born over the edge of the earth.

Some of the young braves whooped and cried out loudly until the older men told them to be quiet. So the young men raced their stolen ponies back and forth at the edge of the stopping place and showed how good they were at escaping the Crow.

Eats-Meat stopped his pony, clutched the sacred bundle across his legs and looked for his father. He heard the low solemn talk among the men. Some of them lay on the ground, examining wounds. Some had blood streaks on their hands and arms and legs.

Strong Rattle, a burly warrior with bulging eyes and a white knife scar across his belly, stood next to his pony, weaving flatfooted. One of his ears was bitten off, and caked blood masked the side of his face. Another brave, Black Crow, worked a flint arrowhead out of his hip. His eyes were watery and the shaft was slick with his blood.

"Did you see that Crow brave lift his loincloth at me?" asked a young man called Hawk Diving.

"I saw him," replied another brave, Makes Thunder, who had seen more than twenty winters. "Did you run?"

"Ha! I took away his eggs with my lance. He squealed like a buffalo calf."

"That is good, brother. I have caught five ponies."

The ponies milled as Rope Earrings made the men pull them all together into a herd. Eats-Meat saw one of the warriors taking count of those men and boys who had made the pony-stealing walk, calling out names.

The young man felt a tug at his heart, as if there were a leather thong tied around it and something was pulling on it. Spotted Dog was dead, so was Blue Frog, another young man, who had seen but sixteen winters, and he heard the braves tell of Swift Panther, who had gone down with six or seven enemy braves tearing at him with knives and warclubs.

So, the strong talk died down and got softer and the brave who made the count, Lean Coyote, told Rope Earrings of those who had gone to the Land of Spirits.

Rope Earrings made three deep cuts in his left arm and cursed the Crow who had killed the three men.

"These Crow were men of bad milk," he swore, so that everyone could hear. "They were women with filthy dresses and they stank of dog. But, we have taken their ponies and we have left their dead in the darkness. Our medicine is strong and we have many ponies to take back to camp."

Two of the men who carried the pipes asked permission to smoke them to make more good medicine, and to sing prayers for the dead. Rope Earrings nodded because he was memorizing his own ponies in the day camp. Most of the others were, too, and Eats-Meat saw his father then, saying strong words to Flying Deer. He shook a fist at the warrior's face and his words carried to Rope Earrings and the others. Eats-Meat jumped off his pony and ran over with several others to see what the trouble was about.

"Why does Flying Deer keep the white pony with his own herd?" Rope Earrings asked, his face hard as a warshield, his cheeks flaring red as if he sweated berry juice.

"Flying Deer caught this white pony. It is mine," said the old warrior.

Eats-Meat looked at the two men as he drew near them, slowed to a halting walk. He could feel the charged air between the two men as if two thunderclouds had struck together and bristled with hidden firebolts. The men stood face to face, their muscles flexed as if ready to do battle and he heard Red Tracks, standing nearby, suck in his breath.

The eyes of the two men did not meet, because that

would have been an open sign to do battle. They began to walk in short half-circles, back and forth, for a little time, glaring at the ground or at the sky, not directly at one another.

"Houhh!" exclaimed Rope Earrings. "You heard the words of Old Lodge. You are to take the white horse to him. It is Old Lodge's reward for making our medicine good."

"No, this is my horse," said Flying Deer. "I will not give the white horse to Old Lodge."

"You will bring much bad medicine to our people. It is not your horse. This was the promise made to Old Lodge."

"Old Lodge is not here. Old Lodge was not at the Crow camp. Old Lodge did not have to fight. Old Lodge did not have to outrun the Crow. Old Lodge does not get the white horse. The white horse belongs to Flying Deer."

For a moment, Eats-Meat thought that the two men were going to fight. But Flying Deer had no lance and Rope Earrings, though he carried the lance borrowed from Old Lodge, still did not look into the eyes of Flying Deer.

Instead, he spat upon the ground and muttered strong words that Eats-Meat did not hear. The words got louder, though, and the boy could hear that the words were bad. He knew that Rope Earrings was insulting Flying Deer without ever mentioning his warrior's name.

"This one," he said, "this one squats to pee like a woman. This one does not fight, but steals. This one does not fight, but runs like a boy whose voice is still high as the loon's. This one will bring bad medicine to our people. This one steals what is not his to steal. This one takes what is not his to take. This one has the bad spirit in him."

Eats-Meat felt the lash and whip of Rope Earrings' words, even though they were not spoken to him, and he cringed like a kicked cur, afraid that Flying Deer would, like a greenwood fire, smoke until his rage became flame and the flame caused him to slay Rope Earrings.

He saw Flying Deer's face grow dark with anger, and he saw a vein in the warrior's neck quiver and pulse like the chest of a frightened bird clutched in the hand.

"I will take the white horse," said Rope Earrings, his voice very stern and loud. "I will give the white horse to Old Lodge as promised. Flying Deer will not steal the white horse from Old Lodge."

"No!" shouted Flying Deer.

Before Rope Earrings could move or say another word, Flying Deer snatched the borrowed lance from Rope Earrings' hand. He swept the lance shaft in a swift arc, struck Rope Earrings hard above the ear, knocking him down.

A loud, collective "hooouuu!", like a sudden gust of wind, broke from the throats of the warriors who stood nearby, and before those who could not see knew what Flying Deer had done, he raced through them, swinging the lance. He knocked Eats-Meat down in his rush, struck Red Tracks in the face with the butt of the lance's shaft and trampled Hawk Diving underfoot. Men and boys fell away from him, like quail scattering from open ground in a hailstorm, as he slashed and struck like a wild man.

He caught up his horses and mounted his pony. He drove the white horse and the others off, away from the herd. He shook the hooped lance in defiance as he galloped away.

"We should chase Flying Deer," shouted Bear Heart. "We should get back the lance you borrowed from Old Lodge. We should get back the white horse. Come. We will ride after Flying Deer. We will punish him."

"No!" Rope Earrings said, as he lurched to his feet and staggered off-balance in a little circle. There was dirt on his back and on his leggings, but he did not brush himself off with his hands. He steadied himself and his face darkened like a thundercloud as he spoke.

"If we chase after Flying Deer," he said, "we may lose all of our ponies. We will return to our people, to camp. We will tell Old Lodge what has happened."

"But Old Lodge will be very angry," said Bear Heart, his cheekbones rouged with the flush of his hot blood.

"We will see what Old Lodge says," replied Rope Earrings, as a lump the size of a prairie chicken's egg grew above his temple. "Come. We must leave this place because we did not get all the ponies and the Crow will be here before the sun moves much more in the sky."

"Hoouu!" many of the warriors grunted.

Eats-Meat jumped to his feet, disappointed. He wanted to go after Flying Deer. He wanted to punish him. He wanted to hit him. He wanted to shoot an arrow into him. He hated Flying Deer for striking Rope Earrings and for taking the lance that belonged to Old

Lodge. He hated him too for taking the white horse that was not his. Surely this would cause the people much trouble. He hated so much he wondered if he hated because this was more bad medicine that could have been caused by the broken arrows and the stolen buffalo hat and the death of Spotted Dog. Maybe those events had caused Flying Deer to do these bad things.

His heart cried out and shouted, but his voice was silent. He wanted to ask his father, Bear Heart, if he was the cause of all these bad things because he had lost the arrows. But Bear Heart turned away from him and caught up his pony. All of the men began to catch their ponies and a rider came in from the direction of the Crow camp, shouting.

"They come. They come. Many Crow."

Eats-Meat's heart was squeezed by his fear and jumped in his chest like a slippery fish breaking the water of a mountain pond. The fear welled up in that place where his heart was and he wondered if there would be more Cheyenne braves left on the ground, their spirits gone like breathsmoke from their mouths.

CHAPTER EIGHT

Some of the Cheyenne braves followed after Flying Deer because he now carried the hohk tsim, the hooped lance. Rope Earrings watched them go and did not say anything. But his face was dark and Eats-Meat knew that his heart was on the ground over the desertion by Flying Deer and six other braves.

"Come," said Rope Earrings. "Let us go back to camp." But, before the band had ridden more than a mile, they heard a man shout.

Eats-Meat turned, as did the others, and saw Winter Wolf, the man who had shouted, go down in a cloud of Crow warriors. The Crow swarmed over him with war-clubs and rode into the rear guard. There were more than a dozen of them, and their shrieks filled the air.

The Cheyenne scattered, and ponies raced in every direction. Eats-Meat shook his lance free of the medicine bundle and turned his pony to meet a charging Crow. The sacred arrows fell to the ground. Bear Heart shouted a war cry and nocked an arrow to his bow. He drew it back quickly and shot an arrow at the nearest man. The Crow swerved and charged straight at Eats-Meat.

Some power inside him rose up and made him hold his pony steady until the Crow brave drew near. Then, Eats-Meat, to the surprise of the other Cheyenne who were near, clapped moccasins into his pony's flanks and charged the Crow. He pointed his lance at the enemy's belly and held the shaft rigid against his ribs.

He shoved the lance hard as the two charging ponies brushed sides, and he felt it plunge into flesh. The Crow's eyes narrowed, then opened wide as the lance went through his belly and came out the other side. The lance wrenched Eats-Meat so that he fell from his pony. He hit hard and little lights danced behind his eyes.

The Crow with the lance sticking through him sat his pony until it stopped. Then, he fell off to the side and made a sound like something falling into wet mud as he hit the ground. The other Crows saw this thing happen and became enraged. They yelled and wheeled their ponies, whipped them toward Eats-Meat, who saw them and started to rise.

Dizzy, groggy, he shook his head to clear out the dancing lights and ran to the fallen Crow, pulled his lance free. Many of the Cheyenne saw this and said to one another that this was a brave thing to do. The Crow was not yet dead, but he made no sound as the lance tore out some of his intestines, broke them open so that their stink stung Eats-Meat's nostrils. He looked at the greasy blue coils, saw them gush steaming from the belly of the Crow. The brave wriggled like a snake, his face squinched up in agony. Eats-Meat, panting, drove his lance-tip into the man's throat, saw the blood erupt like a bubbling spring that comes up out of the earth.

He made a cry in his throat and let it loose to proclaim his victory.

Bear Heart looked at his son proudly, then kicked his pony to meet the charging Crow.

Cheyenne braves called out to Eats-Meat, but his own blood rushed in his ears and he did not know what they said. He jerked his lance from the Crow's throat and turned to face the others. He heard the thunder of their ponies' hooves as the warriors rode at him in a ragged formation that was like the geese flying high in the autumn sky.

Even at that moment, Eats-Meat was impressed with the enemy's horsemanship. The Crow dodged flying arrows, lances, and each man seemed to become part of his horse. The young Cheyenne stood there, transfixed, the fear gone, replaced by a hard knot in his stomach. He found his voice, shouted his defiance at the Crow, exulted in the power he felt surge through his blood, ripple through sinew and muscle.

He began to sing and the song came to him out of his heart.

> *I am here*
> *to kill Crow.*
> *I am happy*
> *to kill Crow.*

It was a short song because the Crow came upon him then, two of them at his flanks. Eats-Meat leaped to one side, aimed his lance at the nearest man. This man now blocked the other one and the Cheyenne who were watching made a murmuring sound in their throats when they saw the boy use this tactic because it was good.

Eats-Meat hurled his lance straight at the chest of the

nearest Crow and as he threw it, he knew his aim was true. He felt his strength, the strength of his arm and shoulder, the strength of his heart, go into the shaft and carry it fast and hard toward the enemy. He yelped a gloating cry as the flint point struck the Crow in the breastbone, bent him over backward.

The stricken Crow fell from his pony, gliding over its rump like a lifeless doll stuffed with grass. There was no blood at first and as the Crow struck the ground, Eats-Meat, like a shadow, leaped out of the path of another who rode down on him like big thunder, screeching a terrible cry that made his heart jump with a sudden rush of blood.

Eats-Meat pulled his lance free and the blood came then, squirting over his leggings, soaking into the earth. The Crow braves wheeled their ponies, tightened the circle around him, but other Cheyenne came riding in, even as Eats-Meat leaped from side to side, dodging the warclubs and the lances. One of the Crow, in a daring move, leaned over the side of his pony and rode over the medicine bundle, snatching it up before anyone could strike him.

He yelled to his brothers, thrust the sacred bundle upward, held it over his head as he rode off in a zig-zag maneuver, one with his fleet pony.

Eats-Meat dashed toward a mounted Crow, swinging his lance, yelling until he was hoarse. The Crow turned, saw the boy coming at him with the bloody lance and nearly toppled from his pony. He wheeled and Eats-Meat met him as he came out of the tight turn, whacked him in the side with the shaft of the lance.

A great cry rose up from the Cheyenne who saw this,

and the Crow warrior screamed in terror, rode off with arrows and lances whistling past him like rain driven before a storm wind.

Some of the Cheyenne surrounded Eats-Meat to protect him, while others chased the scattering Crow, their war-yells and wild yips full of the bloodlust, the hawk's *scree* of triumph. Eats-Meat broke out of the circle of Cheyenne, brushing against a pony, ran after the retreating Crow as if he could catch them, as if he was the wind.

The Crow saw this and one of them cried out in warning to the others. Eats-Meat saw his father pull his bow back and send an arrow in a long arc toward one of the enemy. The arrow struck the man between the shoulder blades and he hunched over, but kept riding after his brothers.

Eats-Meat shouted his joy at this, and jumped up and down as the dust surrounded him, blotted him from view. The Cheyenne yelled and gave chase to the Crow and Eats-Meat started running again, chasing after them, too. He seemed to fly over the ground, bounding like a deer, and his brothers marveled at him, cheered him on.

"Look," cried Big Tongue, "he runs like the sun's shadow when it falls over the mountains."

"Yes," shouted Strong Rattle, whose quiver was empty, "he runs faster than the sun in creek waters."

"He outruns his own shadow," yelled Makes Thunder, making his own comparison.

Eats-Meat heard their shouts and when he came upon Lean Coyote, Big Tongue, and Broken Foot slashing a Crow brave to ribbons, he leaped into the center of them and drove his lance into the man's leg. The Crow screamed and wriggled, turning on his rump in a little circle, trying to avoid the blows of knife and fist.

Broken Foot, a stocky brave with a large, hooked nose, several teeth missing, and a growth on his neck, leaped in close and slashed the Crow's earlobe with his knife. The Crow slapped at the fresh wound. Blood droplets oozed from the cut. The wounded brave snarled at his tormentors, flipped up his breechclout, exposing his genitals.

Big Tongue, insulted, kicked the Crow in the groin, burying the tip of his moccasin in the man's testicles. The Crow's face drew taut and he ground his teeth together in pain. Big Tongue, a man of twenty-two winters, puffed with exertion. His belly was big and round and strained against his sash. His chest bore many scars of the sundance and each one was circled in his color, sky blue.

Lean Coyote, a tall youth, slender, of eighteen winters, cut a piece of meat from the Crow brave's shoulder, slicing it close to the bone. The Crow screamed, then shut off his cry with a stream of profanity in his language. Eats-Meat slashed again with his lance, and drove the point into the man's rump. The Crow rolled over to escape, and the other three Cheyenne danced around him, taunting him with foul words.

"Crow dog," shouted Big Tongue, "you crawl like a whipped cur."

"The Crow eats dog dung," teased Lean Coyote. "Your breath stinks."

"No," said Broken Foot, hobbling up to the Crow and

kicking him in the belly, "you are lower than a dog. You are a lizard crawling."

Big Tongue grabbed the Crow's long black hair and jerked the man's head backward. He twisted the strands of hair so that the man faced his persecutors. Big Tongue spat in the Crow's face and the spittle foamed on his cheek, then flowed down to the corners of his mouth.

Other Cheyenne came over to join in the torment, and one of them was Rope Earrings.

"Do not waste time with him," he said. "Cut the breath out of him and take his hair."

"Cut his heart out," said Thunder Wind, who had ridden up, out of breath.

"Cut off his bulbs and make him eat them," said Red Tracks, his eyes glittering like dark stones under rippling waters.

The men made several obscene suggestions, and Eats-Meat, his passion stirred to a high pitch, threw his lance straight at the Crow's face. It struck him on the bridge of the nose, taking part of the bone with it, as it glanced off. Lean Coyote struck next, dancing past Eats-Meat and driving his knife downward into the Crow's abdomen. His flint blade sank deep, soundlessly, into the flesh, and the Crow doubled up in agony.

Enraged that the Crow brave was still defiant, Big Tongue whipped his blade across the exposed throat, jerked upward on the hank of hair in his fist. The jagged flint edge parted the flesh as if it was a heat-softened lump of bear fat and freshets of blood spilled over the wide cut.

"Aaaiiieahhh!" chorused the watching Cheyenne,

and Eats-Meat felt a thrill that began like a fire in his loins and surged to his chest. The warmth made him giddy and lightheaded as if his own blood had been spilled. Big Tongue, still angry at the enemy brave, pushed the man's head away from him. It struck the ground and the Crow's eyes bulged in their sockets.

Each Cheyenne brave came up, then, and struck the enemy, making room for the next man as the Crow lay bleeding to death from the slice in his neck. Blood pooled up in the dust. There was much of it and it made Eats-Meat's heart glad to see the man dying. He thought of Spotted Dog then, and wondered if he had been tortured like this.

Many Cheyenne kicked the dying Crow, and when the others returned from giving chase to the fleeing enemy braves, they, too, struck the wounded man. Big Heart returned and told everyone he had something to say.

"The Crow have gotten away," he said. "They have taken the sacred arrows."

Many grunted their anger at these words, and none was sadder than Eats-Meat-Quickly. His face grew long and hard as in the moon of December, *Mahk-he-ho-ni-ni*, the moon of the Big Hard Face. Red Tracks looked at him and his face showed contempt, gloating. Eats-Meat glared back at the young man and Red Tracks, seeing the blood on him, backed away, bowed his head in sudden shame.

Rope Earrings spoke then.

"We must go away from this place. It is a bad place for us. We must tell Old Lodge what has happened. We must ask him what to do."

"Yes," said the older warriors, and Bear Heart rode off first, pointing the way to their far-off camp.

No one took the scalp of the dead Crow, but left him there, staring blindly at the empty sky as his body began to stiffen under the bright glow of the morning sun.

CHAPTER NINE

Flying Deer carried the bad and heavy hurts in his heart. He mourned the loss of his shield and his lance. He blamed it all on the bad medicine of Old Lodge. That one had only wanted the white horse for his own personal medicine and look what it had cost Flying Deer.

Now he had the white horse and he had the hoop lance of Old Lodge. These things were his now and they made him feel strong. There were good men riding with him, too, and maybe he could use his new medicine to bring honor to him among his people. He looked around him at the others as he rode, as he worked the captured ponies across the prairie.

Riding a brown-black paint was Double Eyes, and behind him came Long-Legged Elk, who belonged to Flying Deer's own warrior society. Flat Face, the oldest among them, his body wrinkled like the scrotum of a toothless buffalo bull, and Dives Backward, a brash young brave of twenty-four winters who had stolen four strong ponies. His arms were cut where he had taken off flesh to give him good medicine. Now, in the sun of late morning, these were scabbing over like the beginnings of a mud potter's nest. Elk's son, Looking Owl, was light-skinned, had the round, puffy face of his mother, the flattened nose, the large eyes, the small chin. This one had seventeen winters and a bleeding side where a Crow warclub had scraped flesh off his ribs. Snake Child rode hunched over, chanting to himself.

They traveled all that day and through the night. They did not hurry, but kept a steady pace, putting much ground between them and the Crow. Flying Deer looked back over his shoulder during the day, but saw no sign of Rope Earrings and his band, nor did he see sign of any Crow following them.

All through the long night, Flying Deer brooded, his thoughts as dark as the sky. He felt bad inside, felt as if Death were riding with him. He wanted to run his horse, make it gallop until the wind blew away the feeling of death, but he knew that he could not outrun such a thing.

Instead, he thought back to a time when he was a young man, when his medicine was strong. He thought of the time when he was captured by the Crow and made a slave. He thought of the Crow woman, Blue Shell, and the Bear-Who-Helped-Him.

Flying Deer had sixteen winters and was hunting with his father, Striped Arrow, when the people were camped on the Sheep River, what the white men now call the Big Horn. They went on foot into the woods and found two buffalo sleeping. Striped Arrow killed one and Flying Deer killed the other. Both were young bulls and they did not get up from their beds.

"Come," said Striped Arrow, "we will take the hearts and livers back to camp, then come back in the morning for the rest of the meat."

Flying Deer and his father skinned and cut open the buffalo they had killed, took the hearts and livers, covered the carcasses with the hides and carried the organ meat back to their lodge, and gave the pieces to Flying Deer's mother, Blue Shawl.

"We killed two buffalo," said Flying Deer, without thinking. It was not his place to say this thing, but his father did not rebuke him.

"Did they run away after you took their hearts and livers?" she asked, with a wry smile, "or did you eat them both up?"

"We will take horses and get the meat when the sun wakes up," said Striped Arrow.

That night, they brought their horses to the lodge, three of them, along with a pack horse. They tied them up, went to sleep before the moon came over the smoke hole.

But a war party of Crow had come upon the dead buffalo that same afternoon. They knew the Cheyenne were camped down on the Sheep, so they came that way, through the woods.

"Some Cheyenne have killed these buffalo," said the leader of the war party, a man named Hunts Wild Horses. "They will come back for the meat with the next sun. We will wait for them and kill them. We will take their horses and this good meat."

So the Crow made camp over the hill from where the dead buffalo lay and waited for the sun to be born again.

Early in the day of the next sun, Striped Arrow, Flying Deer, and Blue Shawl rode up to the woods. They did not know the Crow were watching them as they cut up the buffalo meat, loaded it onto the pack horse. The

Crow waited until they had finished and were starting back down the slope to the Cheyenne camp.

Hunts Wild Horses and his braves rode up fast and began shooting arrows. Blue Shawl went down, a Crow arrow in her breast. Flying Deer fell from his horse when an arrow struck its belly. The horse kicked and jumped, throwing the young man into some brush. Striped Arrow fought the Crow for a long time, riding back and forth, dodging clubs and arrows, but Hunts Wild Horses finally brought him down, shooting him in the throat. The Crow did not make much noise. Three of them ran up to the brush where Flying Deer lay with a twisted ankle that was beginning to swell up. There was much pain and he had lost his bow and quiver.

"Shall we kill him?" asked one of the Crow braves.

"No, we will take this one to our camp," said Hunts Wild Horses, "and he can be my servant."

"That is good," said Sleeping Owl, a Crow with a humpback.

Hunts Wild Horses had three wives. One of these was a captured Cheyenne woman named Falling Star.

Flying Deer stayed in the lodge of Hunts Wild Horses, who made his Cheyenne slave tend his herd. He could not run away since the other herders watched him all the time. But Falling Star made friends with him and talked to him when the other two wives were not around. They did not like Falling Star and made her work hard—carrying in wood, dressing hides, and making moccasins—all the time. Whenever Hunts Wild Horses was not near, they whipped her with quirts, struck her with sticks, and threw stones at her. Flying

Deer saw these things and it made his heart fall to the ground.

Flying Deer became friends with Falling Star and one day, when they were alone in the lodge, he spoke to her about what was in his heart.

"These Crow women have much hate for you and they treat you like a dog. This gives me anger. I do not want to be a prisoner here. Do you?"

"No, but what can we do? They are many and they watch us."

"You can make us moccasins and hide them. Wrap up some dried meat for us and hide it away. When we have enough, we will go from this place, back to our people."

Falling Star was young and not from his tribe, but he knew she would be taken in by his people if they could escape.

"How will we ever run away?" she asked, a fear-tremor in her voice.

"When the men go after buffalo, this man Hunts Wild Horses will take his Crow women with him. I will go with them, but come back. I will hide my horse and take another one. You will ride my horse and we will go away."

"When will this be?" she asked, for it was winter and the camp was on the Sheep, far below the place where the Cheyenne were camped.

"Maybe in the Big Wheel Moon, *Mah-kohk-tsiu-tsi*, or maybe *Poo-tane-ishi*, the Buffalo and Horses Begin to Fill Out Moon, they will go then to hunt." These were the white men's months of February and March.

So, they remained with the Crow all through the winter and until the snow began to melt in the spring.

"Did you make moccasins?" Flying Deer asked.

"Yes. They are hidden in a place where I found wood."

"Then put some dried meat away too."

"I have done this thing," said the Cheyenne woman.

"The Crow will go after buffalo soon."

As Flying Deer had said, the Crow went after buffalo. Hunts Wild Horses took along his two wives, and the other men took their wives to help with the skinning and packing. Falling Star was left behind with the children and the old ones.

Flying Deer started out with the Crow, but after he had gone a little way, he drifted away from the warriors and rode back to camp. He rode past it to the other side, hid his horse in the timber, and tied him there. Then he circled the camp, caught himself another horse, and rode into camp.

Some of the people who saw him ride in alone were very curious.

"Why are you here?" they asked suspiciously. "We thought you went to hunt buffalo."

"My horse threw me and ran away and I could not catch him," Flying Deer said. "He has my blankets on him."

He went into the lodge, then, and spoke to Falling Star in whispers.

"You must hurry," he said. "Take your things and sneak out to the timber where I have hidden my horse near the creek. I will ride out and circle the camp, meet you there. Wait for me."

He rode from the camp then, to distract the Crow, while Falling Star took her things and stole into the timber. She was waiting for him when he rode up, and she had the moccasins and the dried meat. He tied all the things in blankets and the two rode down the creek.

But Flying Deer did not know that some of the boys who herded horses did not believe him or trust him. These young Crow got bows and arrows and followed the Cheyenne boy into the timber. They rode ahead and hid along the creek. They waited for the two prisoners and when Flying Deer rode up, they burst from the brush and began yelling and shooting arrows. One arrow struck Falling Star, but she did not tumble from her horse right away. Then, another arrow struck her in the back.

"Run!" she shouted to Flying Deer. "Go away. I am going to give up my spirit this day."

The boys shot many arrows at Flying Deer as he rode up and grabbed the hair bridle of Falling Star's horse. He galloped away, pulling her horse, hoping that she would not die. But she fell off her horse and he saw that she was dead. The boys did not have horses, so they did not follow him.

Flying Deer rode on until he passed Pumpkin Buttes, then made camp and lay down to sleep. He was very tired and his heart was heavy because the Cheyenne woman had been killed.

During the night, the horses screamed at the scent of a mountain lion. They broke loose and ran off before Flying Deer could catch them. The next day, he gathered up his blankets and his few things and started tracking the horses. But the tracks disappeared and he began to walk toward his own village on the Sheep.

That night he slept in a strange place and he had bad dreams.

The next day, Flying Deer awoke feeling strange. He did not know where he was. The sky was overcast and it was cold. He could not find his bearings, and he did not know where the river was anymore. He started walking, finding north by the moss on the trees.

He knew something was following him, and when he turned around, he saw a huge bear ambling along, sniffing his tracks. Flying Deer ran until he could run no longer. He collapsed against a tree and saw that the bear had run with him, step for step. He caught his breath, ignored his aching side, and began to walk away. The bear followed. All that sun, the bear dogged his tracks, but always kept the same distance.

Finally, Flying Deer stopped. He turned and spoke to the bear.

"Bear, you follow me. I mean you no harm. I am Cheyenne and I want to get back to my own people." . The bear sat there, looking at him, its tongue lolling over sharp teeth. Flying Deer walked on, and every time he looked back, the bear was still there. The young man's heart beat fast. The bear was so big, and followed so close, Flying Deer was afraid it was waiting for him to drop before it killed him and ate him.

Exhausted, he no longer cared. He could not go on any farther. Flying Deer collapsed. He did not spread out his blankets, but fell atop them, panting from exertion.

"Bear, I cannot go on."

Flying Deer fell asleep, too tired to eat the dried

meat he carried, and in his mind he heard the bear speak to him.

"Wake up," said the bear. "Go to your people. I follow you only to watch over you and protect you from harm. I step in your tracks, cover them with mine, so the enemy cannot follow your trail."

Flying Deer woke up, saw the bear sitting nearby. He was still afraid of it. He gathered up his blanket, the extra moccasins, his bow and empty quiver, and began walking again. Every time he looked back over his shoulder, the bear was still there, keeping the same distance. He walked until the sun went to sleep and then he lay down and slept. In the morning, he looked around, saw the bear up slope from him, squatting on a rotten log, chewing grubs.

Flying Deer started walking, sure of his bearings now, and he was surprised to see the bear come down the slope and begin following in his tracks. That night, he ate his last piece of dried meat.

Early the next day, Flying Deer came to the Sheep and his heart soared. The river was running full and fast from the spring runoffs. He knew he had to get to the other side to find his people. He walked up and down the bank, but there was no way to cross. The waters boiled and raged from bank to bank.

Finally, he sat down and just stared at the opposite bank. To his surprise, the bear ambled up to the bank in front of Flying Deer. Then, it backed toward him. Flying Deer scooted backward, thinking the bear wanted his spot. The bear kept backing up.

"I wonder," thought Flying Deer, "if he wants me to ride him across this angry river?"

Flying Deer got up, walked down to the riverbank to see what the bear would do. He sat down, close to the tumbling, muddy waters. Again, the bear came close, backed up to him.

"Bear," said the boy, "if you want me to, I will get on your back and you can carry me across the river."

The bear tossed its head and waited. Flying Deer wrapped his blanket around his shoulders, crawled hesitantly onto the bear's back. The bear looked back after Flying Deer put his arms around the animal's neck. With a snort, the bear leaped into the river. The bear swam across, stronger than the river's current, its powerful arms and legs enabling it to carry them safely to the other side.

Flying Deer walked north, the hunger in him so strong it began chewing at his belly like a wolf.

The hunger made him lightheaded, and he grew weaker, until finally he stopped and began muttering to himself.

"I am too tired to go on. I am too hungry. I will starve before I ever find my people again."

He was sure the bear spoke to him, even though the sky was swimming around overhead and the ground wavered underneath him as if the earth were shaking.

"Go on, warrior," said the bear. "You will find your people."

Flying Deer lurched to his feet, staggered on. The bear followed behind him. The man got dizzier and weaker, however, and when he came to a little hill, he sat down, too confused to go on. There he saw a creek feeding into the Sheep, and along the creek, a herd of buffalo grazed. Flying Deer's stomach rumbled, twisted. Sharp pains shot through his belly.

"There are buffalo," he moaned, "and I have nothing to kill them with. I am starving to death."

Flying Deer was sure he heard the bear answer him.

"You will eat, brother. Stay here. I will go and kill a buffalo."

Too weak to move, Flying Deer watched as the bear stalked the buffalo. He saw it move through the timber, steal up behind a group like a huge shaggy shadow. The bear moved slowly and crept up on a young bull. Then, it roared and charged on all fours and when the bull bolted, the bear stood up and smashed its legs out from under it. It fell on the bull and bit its spine. The buffalo shuddered and died. The other buffalo ran off.

Flying Deer's mouth watered. He summoned his remaining strength, crossed the creek to the place where the dead buffalo lay. He skinned it, cut it up, then struck flint and steel to make a fire. He cooked the meat and ate it as the bear sat on the hill above the creek and watched him.

When he had eaten his fill, Flying Deer felt stronger. He wrapped much of the meat in the buffalo hide, left the rest.

"This is for you, bear," he called. "Come down and eat."

Flying Deer continued his journey. The bear ate the buffalo meat he had left behind and then followed him. For the next several days, he ate of the buffalo and left pieces of meat for the bear.

Days later, Flying Deer walked over a hill and below

he saw a village. Smoke rose from the lodges and children scampered about.

"I do not know if those are my people," he said.

"Those are your people," said the bear. "Go and tell them that I brought you home safely. I will go into the woods and wait for you. Bring me a buffalo hump that is cut into four pieces."

Flying Deer walked into camp and the people shouted their happiness to see him. He told them about the bear and they got a buffalo hump, cut it into four pieces. The whole camp wanted to see the bear, and a long procession followed Flying Deer into the timber. The people brought gifts: a fine robe, brightly colored beads on a string, hawk and eagle feathers, a wooden bowl made from a burned-out hickory boll, and other trinkets.

Flying Deer gave the bear the meat. The people put the robe around the bear's shoulders, hung the string of beads around his neck, and tied the feathers to the shaggy hair on his shoulders.

Then the people went away and left the bear to eat alone.

Flying Deer remembered these things as if they had happened only a sun ago.

The next sun, when the ball of fire stood straight overhead, making the smallest shadow-puddle under their horses, they came upon a herd of buffalo. The wind was in their favor, blowing in their faces, when Flying Deer halted.

"We are now far enough from the Crows," said Elk. "Let us hunt buffalo and get some meat."

"Yes," said Flying Deer. "We will hunt with the lances. Choose your best horses."

The buffalo herd was stretched out over a long distance, feeding, moving slow across the high grass prairie. Some of the shaggy-headed bulls looked at them with small, mean eyes, and one of them snorted softly, pawed the ground with its forehooves. The Cheyenne sat their horses perfectly still until the old bull tossed its head and went back to feeding on the edge of the herd.

The warriors picked out their best ponies and readied their lances. The buffalo herd moved like a single great body, the backs of the animals rippling like a snake sliding over rocks.

Flying Deer and the others rode up behind the herd, moving slowly, but faster than the herd. They rode up as close as they could before those buffalo at the rear became suspicious and broke up to look at the intruders, first one, then another, until five or six bulls and a few cows stood their ground, blowing steam droplets through their nostrils.

The Cheyenne braves charged then, descending on the herd like leaves blowing before an autumn wind in the Plum Moon.

Flying Deer rode up on the right side of the biggest cow. He held his lance across his body, his right hand raised. When the buffalo was just ahead of his horse, he thrust the lance downward with both hands, pushing forward to outpace the speed of the fleeing animal.

The lance just pricked the animal, and Flying Deer had to poke it again. The hoop would not let him drive it down deep, but he pushed downward past the spine and the buffalo choked, stumbled. He turned it with his horse, then thrust the lance again, in behind the animal's right shoulder. He twisted, cutting an artery to the heart. The cow went to her knees, a blue tongue slithering between its teeth. Flying Deer leaped from his horse, cut the cow's throat with his knife.

He began to cut up the dead buffalo, when he heard the thunder of hoofbeats.

Flying Deer's blood froze.

He looked up, saw the Crow war party riding down on them. He rubbed a bloody hand across his sweat-soaked brow. He grabbed the hooped lance and stood up, prepared to fight, to die.

He saw the bear, then, or thought he did. It sat on its haunches several moccasin steps away, bright feathers jutting from its mane, a robe over its shoulders, a beaded string hanging from its thick neck.

Flying Deer looked away quickly, suddenly shamed. He knew now that he would never return to his own people.

He began to sing his death song. The words stuck in his throat like strangling chunks of dried meat. He looked back to where the bear was sitting. The bear was gone, but a Crow brave sat his horse on the same spot. Feathers stuck out from his shiny black hair, and a beaded necklace flowed over his bare chest. The Crow shook off the blanket around his shoulders and pointed his lance at Flying Deer.

Flying Deer sang the words of his song and they came out clear and true.

> *I am going to die this day.*
> *I am ready to die this day.*
> *This is surely my day to die.*

CHAPTER TEN

Eats-Meat-Quickly heard the men talking as they rode along. He saw that Rope Earrings was following the tracks of Flying Deer and the others who had run away. He looked at the tracks, too, and saw that Flying Deer was not riding back toward the Cheyenne camp, but toward the place where the sun came out of the shadows of night to make morning.

At first he heard only whispers and then the voices got stronger and he knew they were talking about him.

"This one will be a great warrior," said Snake Child. "He will bring much honor to our people."

"He is yet a boy." This was said by Black Crow.

"Maybe he is Sun Runner come back," said Hawk Diving, and Eats-Meat heard this clear, but he did not understand.

"He needs a new name," said Snake Child. "A man's name."

"Yes," said Strong Rattle. "Bear Heart, you have a man-son now. He is Sun Runner."

Eats-Meat heard the talk and it made him feel strange. He felt his stomach boil with excitement and his neck and face grew hot with the rush of blood coursing beneath the flesh.

Rope Earrings himself began to talk to Bear Heart as they rode close together and Eats-Meat saw them both look back at him. He looked away, felt a lump build in his throat until he could not swallow.

Thin clouds of powdery soil rose from the hooves of the horses and the sunlight made the motes sparkle like the dust of a small rain moving across the land. The stench of horse-sweat clogged Eats-Meat's nostrils as he rode behind the loping herd, straining to hear every word spoken by the men around him. He looked at the bobbing rumps of ponies and grew proud that there was so much wealth for his people. He did not understand what the men were talking about, but he felt close to the sky and earth and the dust of travel smelled good to him, like new earth in the spring moons, when the ducks and geese hide the sun as they fly north back to the land of the dancing lights.

The men spoke softer when he was near, and soon they began to ride away from him. He heard no more strange talk during the long ride because he rode alone on the flank of the herd, out of the billowing tail of dust. Once he thought he heard something overhead, like the flapping of wings, but when he looked up, the sun blinded him, brought tears to his eyes. But the skin on his back crawled as if someone had tickled it with the tip of an eagle's feather.

As the sun floated across the sky, Eats-Meat thought of Spotted Dog and the other braves who had died at the hands of the Crow. He wondered where Spotted Dog's spirit was. In the little pictures in his mind, he saw him in the sworl of dust, as smoke, but not smoke exactly, more like the mist of mornings in the summer moons. He thought of him as breath gone away, the breath leaving his mouth, going up to the sky, up to the Spirit World.

An odd feeling came over him as he rode on the edge of the dust cloud. He wondered if Spotted Dog could hear his thoughts, the words that talked only in his mind, not through his throat. He wondered if Spotted Dog's spirit had eyes, if Spotted Dog could see him from someplace in the sky.

His skin began to crawl as if he had rolled upon the earth and picked up mites. It was hard to imagine that Spotted Dog wasn't there, carrying the buffalo hat. It was hard to imagine that Spotted Dog would never be there again to play with him or to talk to him when the lodges smoked with the cooking fires after the sun went to sleep.

He knew from what he had been told that everything was alive and that the spirit of Spotted Dog was part of the air, but not of the air, only something like his breath had gone out of him to the Spirit World. As if that breath part of him had been taken beyond the mountains, beyond the sky. He thought of Spotted Dog not ever being there again, and when he thought this, he also thought of his friend's little body lying out there in the darkness and now in the sun, with the flies eating at the eyes, crawling into his nose holes, crawling into his open dead mouth and down into his throat.

Eats-Meat felt a sudden hurt, like a wind through his mind. His stomach shrank, became like emptiness, then filled up with lifeless air. It was hard to breathe then, and he looked around to see if anyone had noticed the change in him. The flesh on his face felt hot, then cold, and he wondered if the fear in him was because of

Spotted Dog dying like that, with no one to help him, his brains dashed out by a warclub.

He knew that men died. Women died. Animals died. And he knew that their spirits went away and lived on. These things had never meant much to him before, but now he could see Spotted Dog's face, could hear his laughter, could hear his words—words that he would never speak again.

Eats-Meat began to wonder about death, too, and if the old ones were right about it. He wondered if Spotted Dog was happy or if he was weeping because of the way he had been killed, the way his life had been taken away by the Crow.

Was this sadness in him for Spotted Dog a sadness for himself, too? It was a sadness. It was deep and hard to understand. It was a great longing sadness for something that he knew he could never have again. This friend. This boy. This companion. That is why he felt bad and did not feel good about the pony he had taken from the Crow herd.

The wonder in him was great, as great as the bewildering sadness that had come over him like a shadow, like a heavy buffalo blanket in the darkness. Because he wondered, too, if the broken sacred arrows had been the bad medicine that maybe had killed Spotted Dog, that had let the Crow beat the life out of him, the human life and the spirit breath.

"Can you hear me, Spotted Dog?" he asked silently. "Can you see these things in my heart? Do you know that my heart hurts, that my heart is on the ground for you? Do you know these things in my head, Spotted Dog?"

Even as he asked the questions, Eats-Meat felt the presence of Spotted Dog even though Spotted Dog was gone. He would never see him again, yet he felt him in the air, in the scent of the spruce trees, in the scent of loam that filled his nostrils when he breathed, in the sworls of dust that rose up from the earth, in the heady sweat of ponies, and in the oily aroma sleeking the skins of his brothers. He knew that Spotted Dog's spirit was near him and maybe like breath inside him. Maybe he was breathing Spotted Dog's spirit. Maybe Spotted Dog's spirit would help him live just as the antelope meat helped him to live. For his people believed that when you killed an animal and took it for food, this was a gift and one must thank the animal one killed, for all the animals were brothers to that one. That is why one must tell the antelope that someday your own body would feed the grasses that fed him and his family and his offspring and his brothers to come. Maybe Spotted Dog had given him something in his death, had given him breath, making him feel the life he had in his own heart much more keenly.

He imagined then that Spotted Dog was sitting behind him on the pony, riding with him now, and that he had his arms around Eats-Meat's waist. He did not know if there was anything wrong with the way these strange thoughts came in and out of his mind. He did not know if there was anyone he could ask who could answer the questions he had in his heart.

"Maybe, Spotted Dog," he said inside his mind, "you are with me now and maybe you will be with me always. Maybe as long as I remember you, you will be with me."

And these thoughts made Eats-Meat feel good, made him feel not so much alone. Even though something tugged at his heart like a thorn stuck in his leggings, and the emptiness was still there, he knew that Spotted Dog's spirit was not in such a hurry to go to the far land beyond the sky and the clouds. He knew that maybe Spotted Dog's spirit lingered on, like smoke in a long valley, like the mist that rises from the grasses in the early morning when the sun was born again in the east.

The sun threw the shadows of the Cheyenne and their ponies back and stretched them thin as Rope Earrings raised his hand and slowed his horse. Ahead, there was a stream and plenty of grass for the animals. The stream was full of shadows and fingers of shining light where the trees did not grow.

"We will stop here and rest," said the warrior. "We will talk of some things."

When he said this, Rope Earrings' look was on Eats-Meat, and the boy felt strange, as if the warrior could look into his heart and see what could not be seen.

Red Tracks looked at him too, and Bear Heart walked between them, leading his ponies.

"Come," he said to his son, "put your pony with mine and we will watch them so that they do not run away."

"Yes," said Eats-Meat, his throat thick with an unswallowable lump.

When the horses were tied so that they had plenty of grass to graze on, Bear Heart took his son a little ways from camp and they sat down, facing the place where the sun went to sleep beyond the mountains. It was quiet, with only the feeding nicker of the ponies, and the soft low talk of the men as they picked out the places where they would sleep.

Bear Heart did not speak for many beats of the heart. Instead, he looked at the sky and watched the clouds burn with fire until they became lumps of charcoal.

"You have heard us talk of you this sun," the man said, finally.

"Yes, my father."

"Do you understand what was spoken?"

"No."

"You have heard of Sun Runner?"

"No," said the boy. "Who is this Sun Runner? Why do they speak of him? And . . ."

"Listen. This is one story. A true story about a hero of the Cheyenne."

"Is it about the Sun Runner?"

"Do not talk anymore. This story has much in it of magic things and of old times when the Cheyenne had no ponies and they were close to the Great Spirit. After this story, there are more stories about this great warrior hero of our people that I would tell you."

"Why do you tell me stories about this hero?"

"Because many bad things have happened on this steal-the-ponies journey and many good things too. You had iron in your arm when you killed the Crow and some of the others say they saw a red hawk like sunfire over your head this day."

"I do not understand, my father."

"That is why you must listen to my words. That is why I will tell you these old stories that my people have almost forgotten. But you must listen and not throw your questions at me like pebbles onto the lodgeskins."

Eats-Meat felt his blood surge up in him and his belly filled with little buzzing mosquitoes.

Perhaps, he thought, the red hawk, shining like sun-fire, had flown above his head.

As his father began speaking, he felt the skin on his back prickle. He shivered, shook off the sudden chill.

CHAPTER ELEVEN

"Many, many moons ago," Bear Heart said, "before the Tsis-tsis-tas had met the Suh-tai and found that we were cousins, our people did not live on the big river. We were coming to the country of the Red River when we met the *Ho he'*. The Assiniboins. Our people had surrounded a herd of buffalo and so had the Ho he'. We quarreled with them and there was a fight. Our people had only clubs and sharpened sticks to fight with, but the Ho he' had guns and they killed some of our people and took their scalps.

"But a young man who was poor saved us and got us away from the Ho he' before all of us were killed. This young man had a red hawk flying over his head and bullets would not touch him or hurt him. The red hawk protected him and when it flew over him the sun made its feathers so bright they were like the sun and the people began to call this hawk a sun runner because it floated over them like a small sun and they could follow it to safety. The people began to follow the young man, who ran underneath the floating hawk, and finally our people halted on this big river where we now live, the Missouri.

"The young man stood up and said strong words to the people. He was very angry that they had to run away and he had much shame so that his words became like a rain of stones on the ears of the people. He said these things: 'Now we have fought the Ho he'. They attacked us and have killed some of us. After this, let us fight with all the strange people we meet, and we shall become great men.' So our people began to fight all the tribes wherever they met them and we became great. We came to be great warriors and we took many prisoners. When we met the Suh-tai, we fought them, too, but when we heard them speak, we could understand them, so we knew we were related. We made a peace with them and this has never been broken. This has made us strong."

"But what about the young man and the red hawk?" asked Eats-Meat softly. "Who was he?"

"He came to be known as Sun Runner, because he was like the hawk and the hawk was like part of the sun that had come down and floated over the earth. The sun shone very bright on its feathers and you could not look at the hawk without being blinded. You could only see its shadow running very fast along the ground. And some said that Sun Runner himself was the hawk's shadow, because he was very brave and very strong and he could run faster than any man."

Bear Heart was silent for a time and now they could no longer see the dark chunks of clouds that were like char in the sky. Some of the warriors began to walk over to where father and son were sitting. They, too, sat down so that they could listen to Bear Heart tell his son the old stories. Rope Earrings came over first, then Jumping Deer and Broken Foot, Lean Coyote, Hawk Diving and Strong Rattle came together, and Red Tracks and his father were the last to come, until a large circle of sitting men was formed. Makes Thunder sat close to Red Tracks and the two made little sound.

Eats-Meat did not know what to say. He knew that his father had not told him all of the story and he wanted to ask him to go on, but this would have been impolite, so he waited, hoping Bear Heart would speak again.

"We do not know where Sun Runner came from," said Bear Heart finally, "but he led our people away from the guns of the Ho he' and across the Red River and to the Missouri. For many moons we had no guns and we lived in terror of the Assiniboin because they hunted us and would shoot us and take our scalps.

"There are many stories about Sun Runner," continued Bear Heart, "and some say he died and came back whenever the people needed him and some say he never dies but is with us always. Others say he dies and then is born at a certain place to a certain family because he will be needed sometime after he becomes a man.

"I do not know if Sun Runner is alive or dead, or if he has come back, but the stories about him are holy and strange, like the shapes the clouds make sometimes, and the faces in the leaves, the shadows that form when the sun goes to sleep. I do not know all the stories, but Rope Earrings and I have been talking and he told me some stories about this hero of ours that give me much wonderment."

It seemed to Eats-Meat that some of the warriors scooted closer to them and tightened the circle.

He began to look at the shadows then, beyond the circle, and thought he saw dark men standing like silent sentinels, and he wondered if Spotted Dog was out there, a shadow among shadows.

"I wonder, too, about this man," said Eats-Meat, suddenly fearful of looking at the shadows. "Is he alive?"

"Mmm. Maybe," said his father. "It is said that he has strong magical powers and that he came to our people long ago, in the beginning time of people on the earth."

"Was the Sun Runner there then?"

"Some say he was. But he was only a boy."

"A poor boy?" Many of the old stories Eats-Meat had heard told of a poor boy who became a hero of the people. He always liked these stories because they were full of mystery, full of deep things that were important to his people.

"Yes, maybe he was poor. He was brought to poor people, people who were starving, and so he was poor too, because he was also starving. He was called another name then, but after what happened later, they called him Sun Runner because they recognized who he was. Maybe he was the first Sun Runner. I do not know."

Rope Earrings grunted and the other braves murmured to themselves. Only Red Tracks and his father were silent, sitting there in the dark like stones.

"Tell me the story, father," begged Eats-Meat, surprised at his own boldness. But after he had spoken, he heard the men and the boys around him sigh and some of them moved closer within the circle.

"The people," said Bear Heart, "were camped by a little creek and near it a white hawk always stayed, perched on a spruce limb. The Winter Man, who makes the hard-face weather and brings the storm, was camped close by and there was another camp nearby where the bears stayed. Whenever buffalo came near the people's camp, the people would go out and try to make meat. But the white hawk would fly out to the buffalo and screech loudly to scare them away.

"So the people began to starve and they lost the flesh on their bones and became thin as the legs of cranes.

"Even when the white hawk did not scare the buffalo away, Winter Man made a big storm, with much snow and the hard-face cold, so that the people could not go out to hunt. They had to stay in their lodges to keep from freezing to death.

"Sometimes the people managed to kill a few buffalo. But when they did this, the bears would go out and drive the people away and eat all the meat. So the people starved and they suffered hard times.

"In the people's camp there was an old man who was deeply troubled over these things. He also was starving because you could count his ribs and see how swollen was his empty belly. But he thought much about the suffering of the people and wondered if there was something he could do to help them. One day, a spirit voice spoke to him and told him what to do. He went away from the camp and cut a stick. He made it flat on one side and on the flat part he cut gashes that looked like a bow with an arrow beside it. That night he made up a bed in the back of his lodge and threw a robe over the stick just as if it were a person lying there asleep.

"Next morning, when those in the old man's lodge rose out of their blankets, they were surprised to see the robe moving as if someone were lying underneath it. Then, to everyone's surprise, the robe was pushed away and a young man arose from the bed. He held a bow and some arrows in his arms.

" 'Ahhh,' said the old man, 'my son has come at last.'

" 'Yes, my father,' said the young man, 'I have just now come in to see you.'

" 'You must be Bow-Held-Tight,' said an old woman who lived in the lodge.

"The boy did not say anything, but that is what the people called him. One day he went to the old man and said, 'Father, where do you go to hunt for buffalo? I wish to go out and see if I can find some, make meat for our people.'

"The old man pointed to a high hill some distance from the camp. The hill was above a place where the buffalo could drink and find wallows. 'When the young men hunt for buffalo,' he said, 'they always go up on top of that hill. It is a good place to look for buffalo.'

"The young man left the camp and climbed up the hill. After a time, he came back and told his father to tell everyone to get ready to kill buffalo. 'Say to them that your son, Bow-Held-Tight, has found the buffalo.' The young man held his bow and arrows tightly to his body, even when he slept and that is why he used that name.

"The people got ready and then went out to kill buffalo. The white hawk flew on ahead and warned the buffalo by screeching and diving at them, but the buffalo were not scared away. They did not move even when the young man ran among them and killed many of them with his arrows. The people, too, killed many buffalo and they were very happy. They sang songs as they cut up the good meat and laughed for the first time in many moons.

"Soon the bears came, but they stayed on the top of the hill and would not come down to eat the buffalo. They stood on their hind legs, but were suspicious about the boy. They were afraid of him and even Winter Man did not make a storm.

"After the meat had been brought into camp, the young man asked his father, 'How have you people been getting along here; how have you been living?'

" 'Son,' said his father, 'we have not been living well. A big white hawk stays here and scares the buffalo away, and the Winter Man makes bad storms so that we cannot go out of our lodges, and when we do kill some buffalo, the bears come and take the meat away from us. We have tried to kill those bears, but we can do nothing to them. We cannot hurt them.'

" 'I will destroy all these,' said the young man.

"The young man went around to all the dead buffalo and took sinew from their legs. He worked all day, making a long string of the sinews. At night, he was finished and he went to sleep. He left the lodge before the sun was born again, but no one saw him leave. But he came back while it was still morning and told his father that there were more buffalo over yonder, beyond the hill, and they should go out and get more meat. They all went out and killed many buffalo. The white hawk flew over and screeched, but he did not scare any buffalo.

"While the people were cutting up the meat, the boy told them about a bull he had killed. It was way beyond where the other buffalo were. 'Cut open this bull,' he told them, 'and spread its belly open, but do not take a single thing from it.'

"Then the boy went away and the people found the young bull and did what they had been told to do. They did not take anything from the bull.

"The people left, carrying most of the meat back to camp on their backs. They left the young bull there, its innards spread out, its belly propped open. Many birds came and began tearing at the entrails and pecking at the fresh meat. There were crows and eagles, blackbirds and magpies, but the white hawk did not come near. He stayed away, watching, afraid of something. 'He is playing a trick,' he screeched, 'he is playing a trick.'

"But the white hawk could not stand it. He saw the magpies feeding and he landed and hopped near, coming ever closer until he lost his fear. 'Do not eat the eyes,' he screeched to the magpies, 'save the eyes for me.' The white hawk hopped up on the bull's head and started to peck at its eyes. Just as he did this, the young bull reached out and grabbed him by both feet and stood up, holding the white hawk in his hands. It was Bow-Held-Tight."

Eats-Meat leaned forward, straining to hear every word his father spoke. He was caught up fast in the story, drunk on the hisses of his father's words, spellbound by the guttural rhythms of speech. No one around them moved, not even as the moon edged a silvery glowing fingernail over the top of a far hill.

"The boy walked back toward the camp, holding the white hawk, which was screaming and crying, flapping its snowy wings. 'Take pity on me, Bow-Held-Tight,' he screed, 'and let me go. If you will let me go, I will make a great medicine man of you and will teach you all I know. I will go far away from here and live with some other tribe. I will live with your enemies and never bother your people again. Only take pity on me and let me fly away.'

"Bow-Held-Tight kept walking and did not say anything for a long time. Finally, he said to the hawk, 'I was angry at you and I was going to kill you dead. But if you make good the promises you made, I will let you go.'

"But as the boy talked, he was tying the long string of sinew to the hawk's foot and the hawk did not know it was there. The young man let the hawk go and the bird flew up in the air and began laughing at him. 'Ha-ha, Bow-Held-Tight thought he was smart, but I am smarter than he. I fooled him. I tricked him. I hate him!' Bow-Held-Tight looked up and said, 'I trusted you and took pity on you, but now I know what is in your heart, white hawk.' He began pulling in the string and the white hawk flapped to get away, but he came down like a stone. 'Oh, Bow-Held-Tight,' the hawk shrieked, 'I was only fooling. I did not mean those things I said. Give me another chance. Take pity on me one more time.'

"The boy took the white hawk home with him and made him his friend. He tied the hawk over the fire so that the smoke darkened his feathers and the fire put a red burnish on them. The fire burned the hawk's tail feathers too, and that is why the red-tailed hawk is that way today."

"What about the bears and Winter Man?" asked Eats-Meat. "Did they stay there near the camp?"

The young man knew that this was a very old story because he had heard one like it about the raven. But he did not know about the bears.

"The people went out after buffalo again," said Bear Heart, "and when the bears came the people were afraid. They wanted to run away, but the boy, who was now called Sun Runner because the hawk followed him everywhere and was his friend, made them stay. He went up to the top of the hill and shot the bears dead. Then he went to the bears' camp and he found two little cubs. They begged him not to kill them, and he told them he had meant to kill them, but instead he cut the muscle from the calfs of their legs. If he had not done this, there would be no bears today. He sent the two cubs off to live up north where there was plenty of food.

"After that, Sun Runner asked his father where the Winter Man lived. His father showed him and Sun Runner went to his lodge. He lifted the flap and went inside and when Winter Man saw him he said, 'Aha, I have heard of you, Sun Runner. They say you are a very strong man. Well, let's see how strong you are.'

"And Winter Man created a mighty storm inside the lodge because he was afraid of Sun Runner. The storm raged, and snow swirled inside the lodge and it grew very cold. Winter Man cried out and his voice was like the shrieking of the wind down the canyons of the big mountains. Sun Runner had his hawk with him and the hawk flapped its wings and Sun Runner grew feathers on his arms and flapped them like an eagle's wings. The snow was so thick in the lodge that Winter Man could not see Sun Runner. But Sun Runner flapped his wings as if he were in a sweat house, and as he and the hawk fanned themselves the snow stopped falling. The mounds of snow melted under the heat of the beating wings.

"The Winter Man called to his family, 'Run, run. Run, my children, run. He is stronger than we are. He has much power.' They all ran away, but Sun Runner picked up his bow and arrows and ran after them. He killed them all as they ran, except one small one that went inside a deep cave and escaped. Even today, when people go to that cave and look inside, they find frost there. They used to bring hot water and throw it inside, trying to scald the child to death. And Sun Runner told them one day that if they killed that one, there would be no more winter. So the people went away and they lived well and happy for many moons."

Bear Heart grunted and sat back, looking up at the stars. The moon was over them, full and bright then, and Eats-Meat could see the faces of the others who had moved close to listen to the story.

No one spoke for a long time, as if they were all listening for something.

"Bear Heart, my father," said Eats-Meat, "do you think Sun Runner is still alive?"

"My son," said Bear Heart, "I do not know, but I have talked with Rope Earrings and with Strong Rattle and Lean Coyote. They say you are a man now. You have proved yourself in battle. You have killed Crow and you have stolen a fine pony. They say you should have a new name, a man's name, and I am going to give it to you."

Eats-Meat felt his throat constrict as if he had eaten a

poisoned leaf and his mouth went dry as if he had swallowed dust.

"What will be my name?"

"Sun Runner," said Bear Heart, and his voice boomed in the boy's ears like thunder.

Around him, all the men stood up and grunted their approval. Even Red Tracks and Makes Thunder came over and touched the man with the new name and the sound of their voices was like a great roaring of wind that is very far off but coming closer as if before a mighty storm.

When he went to sleep that night, under a tree, the boy kept saying his new name over and over.

"Sun Runner, Sun Runner, Sun Runner," he whispered.

The name sounded good to him and sweet in his ears. The name made him feel strong and brave. The name made him feel like a man, like a brave and mighty warrior who was so powerful even Winter Man feared him.

CHAPTER TWELVE

Their bodies lay bloating in the sun, turning black as burned tree stumps.

Dead buffalo lay strewn around them, stripped of livers and hearts, devoid of humps. Birds had taken out the eyes, and buzzards floated overhead, waiting to return to the carrion.

Sun Runner saw the corpses of Flying Deer and Long-Legged Elk, their scalps taken, their genitals carved away, leaving gaping holes in their loins. The smell of death was sickly-sweet on the air and his mouth tasted of brackish iron like the stones that flashed silver and gold in sunlight.

Strong Rattle chanted the names to Rope Earrings: "Double Eyes, Snake Child, Looking Owl, Flat Face, Dives Backward . . ." All dead, all gone to spirit. Sun Runner wanted to be away from this place of death, this place where Cheyenne braves had been humiliated. There were many pony tracks, and though he looked around, he knew the Crow had taken back the white pony.

"This is a bad thing," said Rope Earrings. "The Crow have taken the hohk tsim of Old Lodge. Come, we must go back to camp and tell Old Lodge of this. Tie these dead bodies to horses and let us take them back for burying."

The ponies bucked and shied away from the dead ones, but finally all the cadavers were tied securely. Black Crow and Thunder Wind roped the horses together and led them so that the wind blew the stench away from the others. Sun Runner was sick from the smell, but he knew the relatives of the dead men would want to bury them.

They rode hard all day and stopped once. Bear Heart and Rope Earrings smoked the pipes and the others prepared the few scalps that had been taken from the enemy. Sun Runner watched as Rope Earrings filled his pipe and lit it, then held it toward the sky, then toward the ground.

"O Great Spirit, bring us good fortune," he chanted. "I offer you this pipe and the smoke so that you will hear."

Bear Heart smoked his pipe and offered it to the sky and the earth, saying, "We give thanks that we are alive and have caught many ponies. Be good to us, Great Spirit, and make us strong."

Lean Coyote and Strong Rattle brought buffalo chips they had gathered and placed these on the ground, while Jumping Deer and Broken Foot made a small fire. Red Tracks brought in dry wood.

"Come, Red Tracks," said Rope Earrings. "I will show you the way we prepare the scalps." It was then that Sun Runner saw the dried ball of hair in Red Tracks' hand. It looked like a small dead animal. Sun Runner felt his face grow hot that he did not take the scalp of an enemy. The ceremony, he knew, was for a young man who had taken his first enemy scalp.

Rope Earrings sat down. Strong Rattle set a buffalo

chip between him and the fire. He took from his pouch
a piece of bitterroot and some leaves of the white sage,
put them into his mouth. He chewed on them and
motioned for Red Tracks to stand in front of him. The
young man held out his hands, palms up, the edges
touching. The Crow scalp fell to the ground in front of
him. Rope Earrings spat on each palm and Red Tracks
rubbed his palms together and waved his hands cere-
monially in the air.

Rope Earrings made a sign to Hawk Diving, who
picked up the enemy scalp and put it atop the buffalo
chip, the flesh side up.

"Take your knife, Red Tracks," instructed Rope Earrings.

The boy drew his flint blade from its elkhide scab-
bard.

"Now, take some charcoal from the fire and rub both
sides of the blade, from hilt to point."

Red Tracks took a chunk of charred wood and rubbed
it over his knife. Rope Earrings took the knife from him
and held it over the scalp.

"May we again conquer these enemies," he intoned,
"and if we do so, I will cut this again in the same way."

Rope Earrings made a cross-cut over the scalp, from
north to south, and another from east to west, each time
beginning at the edge farthest from his own body or
toward the fire, and drawing the blade toward him. The
tip of the blade slashed through the portions of flesh still
clinging to the skin and down to the skin itself, until the
fascia was cut in four sections.

"Now, son," said Rope Earrings, handing the blade
back to Red Tracks, "take the scalp and shave off the

flesh from each quarter, beginning in the east, and place it atop the buffalo chip. Place them in the same order."

Sun Runner watched with envy as Red Tracks carried out that part of the ceremony.

When he was finished, Rope Earrings spoke to Hawk Diving.

"Give him the willow twig."

Sun Runner saw that Hawk Diving had cut a small fresh twig from a willow. He handed it to Red Tracks, who already knew what to do.

"You, Broken Foot, take the buffalo chip away," commanded Rope Earrings, "and leave it on the prairie. But, before you do this, you must ask the *maiyun* to take pity on you. Ask the mysterious ones, the spirits, to help you count a coup."

Broken Foot picked up the buffalo chip and prayed to the maiyun and then walked far out on the prairie.

As soon as Broken Foot was gone, Red Tracks bent the willow twig into a hoop, lashing the ends together with a strand of sinew. Then with more sinew and an awl handed to him by his father, Makes Thunder, he sewed the edges of the scalp to the hoop. He had to make the hoop the right size to fit the scalp or else he would have to stretch the scalp to fit the hoop, cutting short holes along the scalp's edges and parallel to them. But, the hoop fit and he began to sew from east to south, to west, to north and back to east.

Strong Rattle stepped forward, carrying a freshly cut willow pole that was slender, measured six of a man's forearms in length. It was trimmed and peeled and sharpened at the butt, with a notch cut in the opposite end.

Red Tracks fastened the hoop to the pole with some sinew. Then, he rammed the sharpened butt into the ground.

Rope Earrings grunted his approval. The other braves murmured in unison.

"It is good," said Rope Earrings. "Carry the pole back to camp on your left arm. When we return we will talk to the *Hee man eh* and have a dance."

When Broken Foot returned, Rope Earrings told them to mount their ponies. Some of the men urinated on the fire to put it out. They set out, at a canter, running the stolen ponies before them because they did not have far to go before they came to the river. They came to the village before the sun had gone over the mountains. At first, there was joy and laughter as the young boys shouted news of the many ponies coming, but as the women and old men looked at the faces of the returning warriors, there was sadness and shrieking.

"Where is my man Double Eyes?" screamed Little Loon and no one answered her. Her face went dark as a thundercloud and she began tearing her hair out and beating her breasts as she trilled a keening song for her husband.

"He is here," said Bear Heart. "He is dead. Many of our men are dead."

The people swarmed over the ponies that Thunder Wind and Black Crow led into camp and there was much wailing and moaning from the relatives as they looked at the dead men, their faces still bearing warpaint, but swollen almost beyond recognition.

Some of the women began cutting off their hair right away. The wife and sisters of Snake Child threw themselves on the ground and rolled around, screaming. They gashed their legs because the blood of this man had been spilled. Sun Runner watched them and looked at the faces of the small children, who were much afraid because everyone knew the spirits would stay around until the dead were buried and might take part of their spirit with them when they went away on the final journey.

Old Lodge did not come out from his house, nor did Rope Earrings go to him right away. First, the dead had to be prepared. The women, after they had displayed their grief for all to see, took their men to their lodges and began preparations. Fires were lit outside for them to see and there was much wailing and keening as the flames danced high, showering sparks over the living and the dead.

No one wanted to prepare Flying Deer's body for burial, so Rope Earrings, Bear Heart, and Sun Runner, along with two women, Magpie and Wolf Dress, agreed to dress the dead warrior for the final rites.

"He was once a great and noble warrior," said Rope Earrings, "but he has no family, no one to mourn for him."

Sun Runner did not speak to his mother, Corn Woman, because she was comforting the relatives of Snake Child, helping to prepare his body for the travois. He had never seen so many dead at once and the weeping in the camp had set his nerves to rattling like hailstones on a shield. It was good to be doing something instead of thinking about the grief that gripped the hearts of the people.

Wolf Dress and Magpie wore antelope smocks, and their chastity ropes dangled as they squatted over the body of Flying Deer. Magpie was the eldest sister of Broken Foot and she was still a virgin, but had many horses. No man had asked her to marry him because she had a sharp tongue and a mean, pinched face that had been twisted that way since birth. Wolf Dress was a widow with no sons or daughters, barren as the earth above timberline. Her hair was snowy white and she was strong and often helped others without being asked.

The two men stretched the stiffened body of Flying Deer out on his back and cut away his bloody leggings, his breechclout.

"Bring his finest clothes," Wolf Dress said to Sun Runner, who went off to Flying Deer's lodge, glad to be away from the deadness of a man who had brought the people so much sadness. When he returned, he was startled to see that the women had bathed the blood from Flying Deer's body and combed his hair. Flying Deer looked small and dark in the firelight, but the women dressed him quickly to hide his horrible wounds. Bear Heart and Rope Earrings brought robes to lay the body on and laid them beside the dead man. Then, they lifted the corpse onto the robes. The women folded the robes tightly around the body, then lashed it with ropes passed many times around it. Bear Heart and his son then carried the bundle over to a waiting travois hitched to one of Flying Deer's best horses.

Magpie and Wolf Dress went to Flying Deer's lodge and looked through his possessions. Soon, they returned to the travois with an old bow and some arrows in a beaverskin quiver, Flying Deer's pipe and tobacco, and some trinkets they found, flute, rattles, and whistles, carved out of wood and polished to a high sheen. These they wove through the ropes so that they would be with Flying Deer when he was taken to the place of burial.

Others who had prepared the bodies of their dead saddled and bridled favorite horses, hooked up the travois poles. Sun Runner watched with wide, staring eyes, his hunger washed away in the tide of excitement.

"Will they go to the place of the dead this night?" he asked his father.

"Yes, we will all go, but we will not reach that place before the sun is born again. There will be some singing first, but the people will want to take the bodies out of camp very fast because their ghosts might wish to linger close to the bodies."

Sun Runner heard the songs then, coming from the lodges where some of the dead men had been prepared for burial. An old man in Flat Face's lodge sang and prayed to the Great Spirit that created people—*Ma-ka-mai-yo-tsim-an-stom-ai*, the Great Spirit-Making Maker. As soon as the man had finished his chant, Sun Runner saw Flat Face's relatives carry the bundle from the lodge and take it to where the funeral horses were tied.

Many of the women had gashed their legs in mourning. Dives Backward's woman, Deer Road Woman wailed over and over, "I shed my blood because my man's blood was shed," and she looked crazy in the firelight, with her hair cut short and gashes in her scalp. Dives Backward's brother, Holding Four Knives, had unbraided his hair so that it fell over his back like a black cape.

Sun Runner knew that the women would not wash the blood from their legs and faces for a long time and many would mourn at the scaffolds for a sun or two. Some would not come away, would not eat or stop wailing until their relations came and brought them back to camp. He had seen one such woman, Lady Dancing Calf, whose husband had died of a sickness many moons ago, and she still mourned whenever she passed his grave and had to be dragged away, kicking and screaming for her lost mate.

An old man called Crooked Buffalo Horn got all the people together and led the procession to the burial place. The horses moved slowly, the people moaning and weeping as they followed alongside the travois, and the braves carried their bows and arrows and some carried lances. Sun Runner looked at the lodges of the dead, as he passed, and saw that the women had thrown out many things and the small children would not touch them, but stayed away in fear of losing their spirits to the ghosts of the dead men.

They climbed steep slopes in the night, following Crooked Buffalo Horn, who labored and walked very slow, and they kept going across the ridges to the big empty place where the dead were always taken.

When the sun was born in the eastern sky, they came to the edge of the mountain meadow and a great keening arose from the people when they saw the old scaffolds, tattered pieces of hide clothing flapping in the morning breeze. Men who had brought peeled poles erected them among the old ones, and lashed them together. Sun Runner worked on the scaffold for Flying Deer with his father and Rope Earrings.

Long-Legged Elk's body, wrapped in its robe, was placed in a tree, high above the ground. His son, Five-Toothed Bear, shot the horse that had carried the body through the heart with an arrow. It fell beneath the tree and quivered until it died.

Rope Earrings shot Flying Deer's horse (under the scaffold) using two arrows, then cut its throat when it did not die right away.

This was done with the horse of every man who had died, and then the female relatives began their trilling and it was like a spirit wind blowing across the grasses of the meadows and through the trees. The air was thin and the breeze chilled the mourning wives, deepening their grief, because there was no man to warm them, no man to hold any one of them tight in loving arms.

"Where do the dead go?" Sun Runner asked Bear Heart, when they were alone. The smell of tobacco smoke mingled with the reek of the dead, wafted to their nostrils as they stood on a small knoll looking at the scaffolds, the mourners.

"The spirits of the dead men will find the trail where the footprints all point the same way," said his father. "They will follow that to the big road of stars and will come to the camp in the stars. They will meet all their old friends and relatives who live in the camp of the dead."

"Is that where Spotted Dog is now?" asked Sun Runner, his voice a harsh rasp in his throat.

"I do not know, son," replied Bear Heart. "Maybe his spirit is on the star road."

It was then that Sun Runner noticed Spotted Dog's family, all alone, huddled together under an empty scaffold. Atop it was a bundle with the young man's possessions, and below it, a small pony, stiffening in death. It was the pony Red Tracks had said he would give to Sun Runner, the day they had fought on the mountain slope.

Sun Runner drew himself up straight and breathed in deep.

"I want to go away from this place," he said. "It is a bad place."

"Yes," said his father. "It is time to go back. The dead are on their way to *Seyan*. We cannot help them find their way."

Sun Runner knew now that Spotted Dog's spirit had gone on the path where the footprints all pointed the same way. He had the good pony with him and would soon be among his ancestors at Seyan, the camp in the stars.

CHAPTER THIRTEEN

Corn Woman stooped over the clay pot, stirred the buffalo stew with a horn spoon. Clouds of steam rose in the lodge, evaporated at the smoke hole.

"Hiding Shield Under His Robe came here," she said to her husband. "He asked that we take wood to the center of the camp for the scalp dance."

"Yes. We came back into camp without our faces blackened so they knew we had lost men, but we did not do the dance because there were so many dead. Maybe that was not a good thing."

Bear Heart sat in his place on buffalo robes, working on a new pipe. He whittled on the mouthpiece, paring it down, testing it between his lips. The pipe was straight, made in the olden way, from the shank bone of an antelope. He had meant to finish it some time ago, after he had cut off the ends and punched the marrow out, but he had forgotten about it. Now, while they waited until the call from the halfmen-halfwomen to do the scalp dance, he worked on the pipe, making the mouth-end smooth.

His son slept in a pile of robes, exhausted after the long journey back from the burial grounds. Corn Woman's aunt, Wool Woman, slept too, for the long night had been one of anguish for her as well. Though she had not gone to the burial grounds, she had stayed with the young niece of Lame Mule and Sleeping Hawk Lady whose daughter, Runs After Mice, was left widowed by Dives Backward's death.

"The boy brought back a pony," said Corn Woman, changing the subject, for there had been much talk about not having the scalp dance when the men returned. Although the scalps had been given to the halfmen-halfwomen, the grief had been so great that the strange ones did not want to have the dance until after the dead were buried, "and there was dried blood on their skin."

"Yes," Bear Heart grunted a reply.

"Spotted Dog did not return. My heart is on the ground for him."

"I have many ponies now. Good men walk the spirit trail, but we will have a scalp dance."

"Do you have hunger, my husband? There is good strong food for you and our son."

Wool Woman awoke at the mention of food, made a mewling sound as she wriggled to a sitting position, her hair tangled from the sleep, her gums working like the mandibles of a grasshopper.

"I have much hunger," said Wool Woman toothlessly.

"Awaken the boy," said Corn Woman. "Shake him. He has slept all this sun like the dead."

As soon as she had said this, Corn Woman scowled with self-reproach. There was still mourning in the camp, and some who went to the burial place had not yet returned. Most of the lodges of the dead men had been torn down and given away by the relatives. All afternoon, some of the women had marched around the camp, their legs cut and bleeding, their hair shorn, wailing their loss. They carried warbonnets and lances that had belonged to their men and they wept until they had no more tears.

Wool Woman crawled to the robes where Sun Runner slept, shook him. He moaned in his sleep, then arose from his bed, groggy, blinking the sands from his eyelids. He stretched, made a long O sound.

"Eats-Meat, do you have hunger?" asked his mother.

The boy did not answer. Bear Heart stopped rubbing the mouthpiece of his pipe and suppressed a smile.

"Are you awake, Eats-Meat-Quickly? There is food. Will you eat?"

Sun Runner stared at the top of his mother's head, too polite to look into her eyes.

"What is the matter with you, Eats-Meat-Quickly? Did the Crow cut out your tongue? Maybe you were near someone who burned owl feathers and have gone deaf. I have not heard one word from you since you returned. Not one." Exasperated, his mother shook the horn spoon at him, flicking hot droplets of broth into the fire. The fire fluttered and spat, but Sun Runner still did not answer. Instead, his lips flexed with an idiotic grin.

"Eats-Meat-Quickly!" his mother said loudly. "Answer me or I won't give you any food."

"Who are you talking to, my mother? There is no one here by that name."

Corn Woman rocked back on her haunches, shook her head until her braids rattled against her fawnskin dress. She slapped her ears, poked a finger into each one. She looked at Bear Heart whose features were locked in an expressionless mask.

"I think something is wrong with your son, my husband," she said. "He is addled, or maybe he has turned contrary since last I saw him. He acts very strange and I wonder if the Crow did not put a curse on him. Or maybe the spirit people took part of him with them on the last trail where the footprints all go in one direction. Does he not know his name? Is this not my son here, Eats-Meat-Quickly? Surely, you do not think I am the crazy one."

"There is no one here by that name," said her son with mock solemnity. "Eats-Meat-Quickly was a boy who used to live in this lodge. He has gone away, never to return."

The trace of a smile played on Corn Woman's lips as she began to realize that her men were playing a little joke on her. She looked at her aunt and cackled with a sudden glee.

"Ah, what did I tell you, Wool Woman? I told you my little boy would go away and a man would return in his place. Did I not tell you this not six suns ago? And who is this man who takes my son's place? Does he have a name? Or is he to be called Nameless and treated like a poor visitor?"

"I am called Sun Runner," said her son proudly.

A stillness filled the lodge. Wool Woman stopped gnashing her gums. Corn Woman sat back on her genuflected legs and rolled wide eyes as the name her son was to bear struck her senses with the impact of a war-club. Bear Heart sighed deep and his eyes twinkled as he looked at his son. The youth's face was washed clean of paint, his eyes strong as a hawk's.

"Sun Runner . . ." Corn Woman gasped. "I have

heard this name, but it is a hero's name, a very old name, and I do not understand this thing that has happened."

Bear Heart set down the pipe and knife, signed with his hands as he spoke.

"Our son has become a man. He has been given a man's name. Now he is a warrior. He has fought bravely. He has killed Crow and stolen a horse. Sun Runner is his new name."

Corn Woman nodded, looked at her son.

"Sun Runner," she said softly, barely able to conceal her pride, "if you have hunger, we will eat this food."

"I have hunger," Sun Runner replied.

"Good," blurted Wool Woman. "We all have hunger. Maybe so we can eat and fill our bellies without so much talk."

Corn Woman glared at her aunt, and with deliberation, dished up her gruel last, and gave her the smallest portion of all.

Father and son sat in the lodge and smoked before the scalp ceremony was to begin. The women had gone to the river to leave the men alone.

For a long time they sat without speaking. It was their first smoke together and Sun Runner felt tall, as old as any brave in the village.

"I would ask a thing," the young man said, slightly dizzy from the effects of the smoke in his lungs.

"Is it a good thing?"

"I do not know, my father. It is about Old Lodge, this one question and I have one other."

"Maybe you should use your eyes and ears and not make questions out of the emptiness in your head."

"I have not seen what I wanted to know. I have not heard anything."

"Old Lodge is asleep. He is in mourning."

"Has Rope Earrings told him of the hoop-lance?"

"That is your question?"

"Yes."

"No. Rope Earrings will speak to him at the right time. Maybe after the scalp ceremony. Maybe the scalp dance will make the telling easier for Rope Earrings. Old Lodge will be angry and he will blame Rope Earrings for all those dead warriors."

Sun Runner smoked on his pipe. It was the one his father had made. He had thought his father was making it for himself. It was a fine pipe, made from a straight shank bone and wrapped with the ligament from the back of a buffalo bull's neck. The ligament had long since dried, making the pipe sturdy, like one made of stone.

"The other question goes up in the smoke?" Bear Heart said, a half-smile wrinkling his lips.

"It is a question of Seyan. I want to know what it is like."

"Why do you ask this?"

"I think of Spotted Dog and wonder if he goes there."

"He goes there. Seyan is the place of the dead. It is above the earth, in the stars, where *Heamma-wihio* lives. Those who die go to stay with him, except those who have killed themselves. The brave and the cowards alike go there, the good and the bad, as well. All who have died are the same after death. They are all equal."

"Are not the bad punished? Like Flying Deer who turned his face away from us?"

"After one dies there is no punishment for bad deeds. Nor is there any reward for those of virtue."

"How will Spotted Dog and the others get up there?"

"His spirit travels over the Hanging Road, *E-kut-si-him-mi-yo*, the wide star path, until he reaches Heamma-wihio, the Great Spirit. He and the other dead ones will live as they did here, chasing the buffalo, hunting game, going to war. I know of some who have been very sick and thought they were dead. They have gone to this country, but have come back. They have seen the camps of the dead. Sometimes they go right up to the village, but do not enter. They meet and talk with the people coming and going over the star roads, but they never go into the camp of the dead. When they try to go in, they come back to life. I have heard them describe the camps and tell of the white lodges, handsomely painted, the people walking about, laughing and talking, the meat curing on the scaffolds, the women tanning the buffalo robes. It is just like a camp on earth, but all of the people are dead."

"I have not heard of these things before."

"They are not spoken of much."

They heard a sound and saw the tent flap open. A man's face appeared in the opening. It was Hawk Diving.

"Come," he said. "The *Hee-man-eh'* are ready. We will do the scalp dance."

"We will come," said Bear Heart. The flap slapped

back down and the two men put away their pipes, knocking the ashes into the fire pit.

He was glad they had eaten, for the dancing would last long into the night. Already, the firesticks had been taken to the center of the village by all the women and children, and there was a quietness as the people made ready to celebrate the taking of enemy scalps. Yet his father's heart was heavy because he, too, thought of the star trail and those who were upon it. Flying Deer, even. He had been a good warrior, but because the medicine hat had been stolen, and the sacred arrows broken and taken away by the Crow, all their luck had gone bad.

"Come, son," Bear Heart said wearily, as he rose from the blankets, "let us paint our bodies red and black."

Sun Runner looked at his father with excitement. He had kept the fires going many times as a boy, but this was the first time he would join the dancers as a man.

He stripped down to his breechclout as his father brought forth the clay bowls of paint.

Outside, a lone drum began to beat softly, calling the people to ceremony—the dancers, the singers, the old men and old women, and the five Hee-man-eh', the halfmen-halfwomen of which the tribe was most proud.

Sun Runner daubed a finger into the bowl of red paint and began to trace a line down the center of his face as he had seen his father do many times before. At such times, he would sit back in the shadows of the lodge and dream of becoming tall and strong like his father. He had dreamed of someday becoming a warrior, of shedding his baby name like the snake sheds its skin and getting a new name, one befitting a strong and mighty brave.

It was good, he thought, to be a man, to be among men at last.

CHAPTER FOURTEEN

Sun Runner and his father left the lodge as the women were returning from the river, carrying water and more wood for the lodge fire.

"We will prepare for the dances," said Corn Woman, proud to see her men painted red and black. She made eyes at her husband and he brushed her away with a smile.

"You are too lazy to dance much," he joked. "Maybe you would like to do something else."

"Go away with your talk," she said. "Come, Wool Woman, let us put on our fine dresses and show these men how well we dance."

"Come, my father," said Sun Runner, impatiently, slipping his ceremonial robe over his shoulders, "I see the Hee-man-eh' putting the scalps on the poles."

Bear Heart grunted and the two women disappeared into the lodge. As the men walked away, they heard giggles and loud tittering. Sun Runner snorted and made a face that was like the opossum's when it smells a skunk.

The Hee-man-eh' were special people to the Cheyenne. They usually dressed like old men and stayed to themselves, and were revered by the tribe. They were halfmen-halfwomen and all belonged to the Oumsh,

Oak, family. The family was called *Otto-ha-nih*, "Bare Legs."

The five Hee-man-eh', Hiding Shield Under His Robe, Wolf Walking Alone, Bridge, Buffalo Wallow, and Big Horse, walked in procession beyond the village circle. There, they attached the Crow scalps to poles. A crowd of small boys followed them, jabbering and poking one another, rolling and tumbling, as they flocked to the place where the strange ones would pretend that the village did not know about the scalps.

"Our shock was great," said Buffalo Wallow, as the others lined up, "when our brave warriors returned from the pony raid. We did not take the scalps because there was much mourning. Now, we announce that our men brought back good Crow scalps and counted many coups. Come, let us surprise the village with the news."

The five men gave a great whoop and raced to the center of the village.

They shouted, "We bring enemy scalps. We will do the scalp dance."

The villagers, pretending to be surprised, cheered the men on, laughed to hear their odd high-pitched voices that sounded halfman, halfwoman.

"We are women. We are men. Watch out women, for your husbands. Watch out men, for your wives."

The people laughed at their joke and it seemed to Sun Runner that a great gloom lifted off the camp. Everyone loved these men who had taken up the ways of women. He liked, especially, Hiding Shield, because he was the sweetest talker of them all. He was the one Bear Heart had sent to Corn Woman's relatives to ask if he might send her gifts. He was the one who arranged the courtship many moons ago.

The halfmen-halfwomen ran around the village, making jokes and proclaiming the number of scalps they had and invited everyone to the center of the village. Groups began to converge there, the women dressed in fine dresses, the men painted black and red. There was laughter and good talk.

All that day, the halfmen-halfwomen had visited each lodge and asked the owners to send firewood to the center of the village. Then, the Hee-man-eh' had built the wood up, piling it in the shape of a great lodge by standing the sticks on end. And all about it and beneath it, they put clumps of dried grass.

"Come see the 'skunk' burn," Big Horse shouted, and everyone knew what he meant. The people called the woodpile *kha-o*, skunk, and it was a big joke to them.

Now, as the sun went away to sleep in the west, the singers with their drums marched to the center of the village where all the people were gathered. The singers were all married men, of many moons. They were dressed in good buckskins, with many beads and scalp-locks attached to them, and they wore the feathers of birds, eagles, hawks, ravens, in their hair.

Sun Runner watched as the old women took up their places, their bodies blackened with soot-paste from the waist up. The older people had their faces and bodies painted black with berry juice. He took his place with the young men as they stood in a row facing north. Across from them, the young women made a row facing the young men to the south.

Then, the old men and the old women took their

places at the lower end of the young people's rows and faced to the west. The Hee-man-eh' took their places in the center of this square of people and Sun Runner knew they would be the managers of the dance. No one was allowed to go where the halfmen-halfwomen stood.

Sun Runner noticed a commotion in the girls' line across from him. A young maiden ran from the middle of the line to a place directly opposite him. She looked coyly at him and smiled. She bowed her head and batted her eyelashes at him until he blushed, his neck burning as if he had been touched with a clump of stinging nettles.

He recognized the girl, then. She was Little Redbird, the daughter of Walks At Night, also called Wrinkled Wolf, and One-Legged Crane. Walks At Night was visiting his Oglalla relatives up on the Big Horn and had been gone for two moons. Little Redbird often helped her mother dig roots and he had noticed her at such times, but he thought she had never noticed him.

Now, in her white buckskins, beaded moccasins, her hair in long dark braids, Sun Runner felt his heart leap like a hawk taking wing. He heard a sharp cry from one of the children, and turned to see Big Horse light the "skunk." Before he could regain his former composure, the women began to dance toward the center of the square. The young men walked quickly behind the drummers to the girls' side and stood behind their sweethearts. Sun Runner smelled the sweet oils in Little Redbird's hair and heard the throb of drums, the croon of the singers as she presented her arm to him. He placed his arm through hers and they danced in a circle with the others. He hardly noticed Red Tracks and his sweetheart, Golden Quail, who danced opposite him. Red Tracks made a snicker, but Sun Runner felt the softness of Little Redbird's arms and was deaf to all but the music, the stamp of moccasined feet on the earth.

Following the "Sweetheart's Dance," the boys and girls returned to their places and stood as before. The halfmen-halfwomen then danced before the drummers, holding the poles with the scalps attached and waving them so that the scalps looked like dark birds in a mating flight. The old men whose sons had counted coups on the Crow danced also, and some were dressed like the enemy and joked with the people, tried to make them laugh as they skipped by on first one foot, then the other, in time to the beating of the drums. Some of the old women, too, began to act like fools, making terrible faces and pretending to be idiotic Crow braves.

Then, the music stopped and, after a brief while, began again. The singers sang the songs of the "Matchmaking dance" and people began to laugh. Sun Runner's knees began to tremble as Wolf Walking Alone and Buffalo Wallow separated from the other halfmen-halfwomen. Wolf Walking Alone went over to the row of young women and Buffalo Wallow came to the line of young men.

"Which woman do you want for a partner?" he asked each young man. Wolf Walking Alone asked the women which man they wanted. Then, the two men met in the center and discussed what they had been told. The singers and drummers were still singing the matchmaking music, stamping their feet in time to the music.

Buffalo Wallow and Wolf Walking Alone took each man and put him next to his sweetheart. Sun Runner had to stand by Little Redbird and wait until each boy had been matched up with his sweetheart.

The women who had their partners danced toward the center and back, not turning. Then, the two halfmen-halfwomen stepped in between the rows and told the young men, "Go back to your places."

The singers and drummers rested as the little boys threw more wood on the fire until the flames leaped higher, sending dazzling bronzed sparks into the pitch sky. The halfmen-halfwomen called for a third dance, and Sun Runner picked Little Redbird for his partner again. They danced as before, then formed a ring around the fire and danced in a circle. The singers and drummers joined the circle and they all danced left about the fire. The old men and women stayed in the center of the ring waving the scalps. They poked the scalp poles at the little children, frightening them away from the dancers. After a while, the halfmen-halfwomen made the girls drop out and only the young men danced the round dance. Sun Runner, Red Tracks, and some of the other young men slipped out once in a while to tease their sweethearts. Sun Runner put his arm around Little Redbird's neck and she smiled at him so that he felt something melt inside him like bee's wax. They danced around the fire until the halfmen-halfwomen ordered them back to their places.

The Hee-man-eh' called the "Slippery dance" next. The singers chanted to the rhythm of the drumbeats. Women, in pairs, approached the men they liked and took away their robes, then danced back to the center, leading the young men to follow. The women would not give back the robes until the men's sisters had given them presents from their sweethearts. Sun Runner had no sister, but was surprised to see Corn Woman, cackling like a prairie hen, present Little Redbird with a pretty bracelet. The girl flicked her eyelashes at him and "set him free" by giving him back his robe.

"Go and rest awhile," boomed Hiding Shield Under His Robe, and the dancers broke from their lines.

"Bring water for everyone," shouted Big Horse, and a flock of little boys and girls scurried away into the darkness to fulfill their mission.

Sun Runner slipped his robe over his shoulders, watched as Little Redbird walked to a place between two lodges with three other girls. One of them was Golden Quail, Red Tracks' sweetheart. He heard them talking, their voices musical on the night air. Little Redbird began to tie up her buckskin dress to keep from tripping on it in the next dance, which was to be a stooping dance. This was the last dance of the evening and was called "The Galloping Buffalo-Bull dance."

"Do you like that boy?" Golden Quail said to Little Redbird.

"Which boy is that?"

"You know. The one with the crazy mother and no sister."

"Do you like Red Tracks?"

"Yes. He is very strong and handsome."

"Well, I do not know if I like my boy or not. He is so young."

Sun Runner's face sagged and he felt his heart sink in

his chest. He wanted to run away, never see the girl again.

"He will grow up," said Golden Quail. "I would like him if he were my sweetheart. But Red Tracks does not like him. I think he is afraid of him."

"Well, I'm not afraid of him. He is just a young man and I don't know if I will keep his bracelet or not."

Little Redbird spoke in a loud voice as if she wanted Sun Runner to hear her. He did not understand why she did not like him. If she gave his bracelet back, which his mother had given without his knowing, he would probably run away somewhere and never come back.

He walked away from earshot of the girls because he did not want to hear any more talk that made him feel bad. He looked over at Little Redbird and saw that she was looking at him again, in that same way. Then, she made a little sign, a circle around her heart and his knees went weak, buckled. He stumbled and nearly fell. He looked away quickly, and regained his balance so that he would not look like a fool. Now, he was more confused than ever and he wanted to take Little Redbird and shake her, or pull her braids until she cried out.

His heart hurt and soared like a hawk at the same time. This was terrible, having such a sweetheart. She was fickle and she was mean, but when she looked at him in that way, with her pretty brown eyes, his stomach fluttered as if it were full of tickling feathers and his loins warmed with a strange heat that made him giddy.

"Everyone sit down," said Hiding Shield Under His Robe, jarring Sun Runner out of his confused reverie.

The people all sat down, even the singers and drummers. "This is the last dance. Drummers and singers, begin."

The drummers thrummed the hides and the singers began to sing. Four women arose and danced toward the men, stooping and bowing. When they drew close, they stooped way down and turned their backsides to the men. They danced in place, until the men began to rise up and dance with them. The men stooped like the women. A few rose up, then more, until all the men and women were dancing together, humping up and down like a galloping herd of buffalo.

Little Redbird danced for Sun Runner and he felt his heart take wing. He danced for her and she laughed merrily as she bobbed and stooped, twirled and bounced. They danced around in a circle when the halfmen-halfwomen told them to, and they were joined by the drummers and singers until the music of the camp filled the air and the patter of moccasins made a sound like the wind. The moon floated over them and drifted off toward the morning sky and as the halfmen-halfwomen danced among them, the waving scalps were seen overhead, flying like nightbirds.

Gradually, the people began to drift away, toward their lodges as the light paled the sky in the east. Little Redbird bowed quickly to Sun Runner and brushed against him, flashing her bracelet in his face. He watched her trip away and felt the tangled rush of emotions flood his senses like blown leaves in an autumn gale.

The dance was over, the dancers gone, and Sun Runner lingered in front of the lodge for a long time, thinking of the girl and seeing her pretty face in every star.

He heard a cough, muffled voices from within the lodge. The edge of the world was turning to fire when he lifted the flap and ducked through the opening.

Sun Runner crawled to his blankets, threw off his robe, and lay on his back, unable to sleep. He was worried. He did not know if he wanted to have a sweetheart. If this was what it was like, he would rather be a halfman-halfwoman or a Contrary.

Finally, he would like to slap Little Redbird's face and tell her bad things that would make her hurt inside.

"Did you enjoy the dancing, Sun Runner?" whispered his mother.

Her voice startled him.

"Yes. Maybe."

"She's very pretty, your sweetheart," she said.

"Very pretty," echoed Wool Woman.

"Go to sleep," gruffed a sleepy Bear Heart. "All of you."

"She will make a fine wife someday," Corn Woman sighed, as she turned over in her blankets.

"*I hate her,*" Sun Runner muttered and stared upward through the smokehole at the dimming, fading stars as the morning sun washed them away with light.

CHAPTER FIFTEEN

Sun Runner awoke, late in the morning, when the sun was almost directly above the smokehole, to find the lodge empty, and the muffled sounds of talking men outside. He shook the moss of sleep from his head and arose from the blankets. Much of the paint had rubbed off during the night, but his skin was still smeared with red and black blotches.

He crawled through the door flap, stood up. Bear Heart and Rope Earrings stood a few paces away, gesturing, speaking slow. They did not notice him at first as he walked up to them.

"Did you tell Old Lodge about the hohk tsim?" asked Bear Heart, his voice a husky whisper.

"That was the thing I told him last."

"Did his heart fall to the ground?"

"He told me that he knew these things had happened, that he had seen the hohk tsim taken away by the Crow. He said that he had seen the white horse and Flying Deer."

"This is a very strange thing to hear."

"Old Lodge told me to go away and there is no sound from his lodge."

"Maybe he is making medicine," ventured Bear Heart.

"Maybe he is talking to the spirits."

"No. We would hear him, Rope Earrings. We would hear his voice through the hides of his lodge."

Bear Heart stopped talking as he noticed his son standing there, listening to them.

"Go to the river," he said, "and rub off the paint."

Sun Runner ran to the bank beyond the camp circles and saw people there, washing off paint, taking water for the lodges. Corn Woman and Wool Woman were with a group of old women. They, too, were talking of Old Lodge in sharp, bewildered tones that were loud whispers, but carried to his ears in the morning air.

The young man plunged into the waters and felt the cold lance him. He splashed and rubbed at the paint on his body as he wallowed in the shallows where the big river made a bend. Small boys played on a sandbar not far from him, making turtles and frogs out of the mud.

Sun Runner floated toward the sandbar, urinating in the water, scooped up a handful of the fine grit, and scrubbed his face and arms until the water swirled with the colors of the paint. He rubbed his belly and then climbed, dripping, from the river, his breechclout weighted with the wetness. He flattened his long hair, slicked it back with both hands. Then he wrung out his breechclout as he stalked back to his lodge, barefoot.

His father and Rope Earrings were not there. Sun Runner put on his moccasins, began to look for them. Many who had danced the night before were still asleep and even the dogs were quiet. He saw few people as he ambled toward Old Lodge's house.

Even before he reached there, he heard the faint song, and though the sun was drying his skin, the fine hairs on his neck bristled and he felt a chill ripple up his spine as if stroked with a feather.

There, standing before Old Lodge's tipi were his father, Rope Earrings, Hawk Diving, Strong Rattle, and Makes Thunder. Their faces were solemn and they stood there stiff-legged as cranes, listening to the singing of Old Lodge.

Sun Runner stood a little distance away, his senses prickling like a porcupine's quills as the song wafted to his ears.

Old Lodge was singing to the spirits, calling to them:

> *My village is mourning.*
> *I am mourning our dead men.*
> *I sing to the spirits,*
> *I call to the spirits.*
> *Hear me, hear my song.*
> *Tell me about my hohk tsim.*
> *Tell me what is happening to my people.*
> *Tell me why our medicine is bad.*
> *Hear my words, you spirits.*
> *Come to my lodge. Talk to me.*
> *Tell me what will happen.*

Then, it was quiet as Old Lodge stopped chanting. The men waited, and shifted from foot to foot like standing buffalo, and Sun Runner wondered if the spirits had come to Old Lodge, were talking to him. He strained his ears to hear, but it was quiet and his breathing was the loudest sound he heard.

"He talks now to the spirits," said Makes Thunder.

"We will wait," said Bear Heart and the other men nodded. Some other braves, their bodies sleek with

river water padded up and joined the group who
waited by Old Lodge's house, and they still looked
sleepy and puzzled by what they had heard. Soon, the
camp was abuzz with the news of Old Lodge's singing
prayers as men came and went from the group. But
most of the people stayed away from the lodge and
waited to see what would happen. Sun Runner knew
they all dreaded hearing what Old Lodge would have
to say when he finished talking to the spirits. So many
bad things had happened, everyone was worried and
no one wanted to talk about it. The medicine arrows
were broken and gone. The sacred buffalo hat was
gone. And, maybe worst of all, Old Lodge's hooped
lance, the hohk tsim was gone, stolen by the thieving
Crow.

Soon, as the sun made the shadows bunch up small
under the moccasins, they all heard a loud wailing from
Old Lodge's tipi. Then, some heartbeats later, the flap
rattled and Old Lodge appeared, tall and stately, a single eagle feather dangling from his scalplock, naked
except for breechclout and moccasins, not even a robe
about his shoulders. His body gleamed with a sheen of
sweat and his eyes were red-rimmed, flashing with a
deep anger that was like the slashing of a knife.

He looked at the men standing before his lodge and
he lifted one hand and made a sweeping motion, then
the talking sign, saying he would tell them all this thing
he wanted to say.

The men were very quiet as Old Lodge cleared his
throat. His chest swelled with air and he spoke in a
voice that sounded as if it came from a dark cave.

"I called the spirits," he said. "The spirits heard me

and they came down to my lodge. They spoke to me. I asked them many things and I asked them about the hohk tsim. The spirits told me that the Crow women and children were abusing my lance and that the lance wants to come back to me. The Crow are playing with the lance as if it were a toy. They are using it to play stick and ball and they are cursing it. The Crow women are using it to punish the children and dragging it along the ground. They are speaking insults to it.

"Send a talker through the village and tell the people this: They must go to the south end of camp and stand there in a line facing east. All must go—men, women, and children."

Old Lodge folded his arms as the men selected Strong Rattle to cry the message to all the people. Then Old Lodge went into his house. He returned after many beats of the heart, wearing his robe, the hair side in. He started for the south of camp, and those who had been listening to him fell in behind him and followed.

All the people of the camp, some still rubbing the grit of sleep from their eyes, some still wet from the river, all gathered at the end of the last circle of lodges and formed a long line from the river to a far place on the prairie. Sun Runner was startled to see so many people in one single line, all gathered to see what Old Lodge would have them do.

Old Lodge stepped in front of the long line of people and removed his robe for all to see. He turned it inside out and put it back on, the hair side out. Then he walked up and down the line singing a strange song.

My hohk tsim wants to come back to me.
My lance does not like the Crow.
My lance wants to come back to our people.
Wind, bring the lance back to me.
Wind, carry the lance to me.

Soon after he began walking and singing, as all the people looked toward the place where the sun was born, they saw a speck of dust, like smoke, in the distance. Then, the dust became a twisting whirlwind, and it danced across the prairie, coming toward them. The people all sighed and moaned and pointed toward the whirling column of dust.

Old Lodge walked away from the line of villagers, going east, out to meet the whirlwind. It was a big whirlwind, like a cyclone, and the people all felt its hot breath as it drew near. Then it grew small, and it raced toward Old Lodge, who stood there, waiting, his robe bristling in the gusts of wind.

Just as the whirlwind of dust came near, Old Lodge dropped his robe and stood in its path with his hands stretched out. The whirlwind rushed toward him and as it passed, he reached inside and snatched out the hohk tsim.

The people cheered until they were hoarse as the whirlwind veered sharply and disappeared over the prairie. They all rushed out to Old Lodge and crowded around him, eager to see the hooped lance that the whirlwind had brought back to him.

Old Lodge held it up over his head, so that all the people could see.

Sun Runner saw it, and still he found it hard to believe it. But that was the hohk tsim that the Crow had stolen from Flying Deer, who had stolen it from Rope Earrings. Most of the feathers were gone and it had scars on it from abuse.

"We will bring beads and give you new feathers for the lance," said Corn Woman. The people all nodded and muttered assent. Many rushed away to gather new decorations for the lance, and Old Lodge drove it into the ground so that all could see it standing. Soon, there were many offerings piled around the lance.

Old Lodge made a sign and the people fell back to listen to him.

"The hohk tsim is back," he said. "The spirits have told me it would come back. But this is a bad time for our people. The sacred buffalo hat is gone. The sacred arrows are gone. Soon, the Cheyenne will know no peace and there will be much trouble for us. I do not know what will happen, but we will be like leaves driven before the wind, and we will be scattered all over the land without a home or a place to camp or hunt. I know these things. The spirits told me these bad things and my heart is on the ground for them. I have the lance back and we must make new medicine arrows and a sacred buffalo hat. But these things will do no good, for the time of the Cheyenne is almost over. Something bad will happen because of losing these sacred old things that brought us good medicine."

Sun Runner felt as if his heart had stopped beating. He was very afraid. He was bewildered. He did not understand what Old Lodge meant, but he saw the sad faces of his people and it was as if a hand had squeezed his heart and made it stop.

Many of the women began to weep and the children looked up at them, puzzled, and pulled on their chastity cords or their skirts.

Sun Runner wanted to shout at Old Lodge and ask him why he said these things.

But his heart was stopped like a dead man's, and the words died in his dry throat. A shadow passed over him and he looked up.

Screeee! Screeee! cried the hawk as it hovered high above him.

And then the golden bird folded its wings and dove straight for him, its talons outstretched. Sun Runner brought his arms up to shield his face and the hawk extended its wings and drenched him in shadow, blocking out the sun for a moment. Just before it struck, Sun Runner closed his eyes.

"What is the matter with you?" said his mother, grabbing his arm. "Why do you cringe? Is the sun blinding you? Are you sick?"

Sun Runner opened his eyes. He touched his face, felt no pain, no blood.

He looked back at the sky, winced at the bright sunlight.

"Did you not see the hawk?" he asked Corn Woman. "Did you not see him diving at me?"

"No," she said. "There was no hawk. You have been in the sun too long. Come, let us go back to the lodge and take food."

But Sun Runner stood there after his mother went away, entranced with his strange vision. Old Lodge came up to him and looked at him; spoke to him in words and handsign.

"The spirits spoke of you, Sun Runner," he said. "They say your medicine is strong, but some are jealous of you. They say they want you to be with them."

"When?" Sun Runner swallowed air.

"Come, let us walk onto the prairie, away from the people."

Sun Runner felt his chest constrict as if wrapped with wet hide strips. He walked with the seer, and they went away from the lance and the people around it. When they were some distance away, Old Lodge reached down and picked up a handful of dirt. He let the grains slide through his fingers, watched as the breeze blew it away, blew it to dust.

"All of this land here belongs to the Cheyenne," he said. "In fewer than twenty snows, there will be strangers here, soldier-people with faces that have no color in them. With skin pale as tanned buckskin. All of the tribes will come together, Lakota, Cheyenne, Arapahoe, even our enemies the Crow will be as brothers.

"But this joining together will not be enough to keep our blood from flowing into the earth. The people will all die and take to the spirit trail in the stars. There is nothing anyone can do to stop this. But you will be brave and will die in a strong battle. That will give us life for many moons because your spirit is so strong it will stay with us. Forever."

"I will fight these soldier-people. I will kill many," said Sun Runner defiantly.

"Yes. This is so. But when you see these people with faces that have no blood to make them red, you will become a shadow. The spirits have told me these things.

"No more than twenty snows, Sun Runner, and you will become shadow. Twenty snows."

And Sun Runner knew that Old Lodge spoke the truth. A great sadness welled up in him as he looked back at the dark clusters of people around the hohk tsim. His eyes brimmed with tears, not for himself, but for the people.

"Is this because I lost the sacred medicine bundle?" he asked, his voice quavering with futile rage.

"No, young man," said Old Lodge, touching Sun Runner's arm, "but that is why we lost the good medicine things. Those things were taken from us to make us see, to make us prepare for what will happen to us."

"Can you not bring the arrows and the buffalo hat back to us like you did the hohk tsim?"

"No. Never," Old Lodge replied. "Come, let us walk back to the people and speak no more of these things."

"How will I know when I am to become shadow?"

"Maybe Walks At Night will give you a fine white horse that is like the one Flying Deer took away from me."

"Walks At Night? He is the father of Little Redbird. He is not here."

"He will come back. You will become his son-in-law."

Sun Runner walked back with Old Lodge in a daze. Then the old man left him and he was alone. He looked at the ground, saw the flutter of a small shadow. He peered upward, to the sky, and there was the hawk, wheeling in the wind currents, silent as a thought. Then, it flapped hard, flew away, its shadow running fast on the ground until it disappeared, like smoke, like steam breath in the snow moon.

CHAPTER SIXTEEN

Five snows passed before Sun Runner took himself a wife. He courted Little Redbird for all those snows and even asked her to run away with him, but she always said, "No, I cannot do it this sun. Let us wait another while when it will be better for us to do this."

Finally, Sun Runner sent the Contrary Lightning Lance, a man who did everything contrary, or backward, to speak to Walks At Night, Little Redbird's father. But Lightning Lance was refused because he got his words mixed up and was no longer good for such things. In a fight with the Pawnee, two winters before, he had been struck by the enemy and some said his brains were taken away.

So Sun Runner waited until the people went to the Smoky Hill River country where the hunting was good. There, the people were happy and there were plenty of buffalo and much meat.

"Will you be my woman?" he asked Little Redbird when the sun was making the shadows long. "I am tired of waiting. Red Tracks is already married and his woman, Gray Plover, is swelling with child."

Little Redbird, who had become more beautiful than any maiden in the village, surprised him when she replied, "Why don't you send a very respected messenger to my father? Lightning Lance brought him four dogs instead of four horses and he made my father angry. He did not think you were serious."

"Lightning Lance is my friend."

Little Redbird pouted and made her eyes flash like polished beads in the sunlight. The two were sitting on a little hill near the pony herd, in plain sight of the camp. She got up and stamped her moccasined foot on the ground.

"Oh, Sun Runner, do you really want to be my husband? You are like stone. Your head is stone. Your eyes are stone. My heart beats fast for you and you wait and wait until sometimes I think you want to be a Contrary yourself."

"No! Do not speak this way, woman. I will send a good messenger this sun."

"Good," she snapped, flouncing away from him, "and you send my father good gifts or he will turn his face away from you."

Sun Runner stood there a long time, angry at her for speaking like that, but wanting to take her for his wife so bad he made up his mind to either marry her or run away with her.

Corn Woman tied six fine horses in front of Walks At Night's lodge, then went inside and spoke to him.

"Walks At Night," she said, "there is such a young man, who is called Sun Runner. He wishes to have your daughter, Little Redbird, for his wife."

She did not wait for an answer, but departed, leaving the horses tied in front of Walks At Night's lodge.

Sun Runner paced and fretted so, after that, that his mother chided him. "Do not worry, my son. If her father will not let her marry you, he will cut the horses loose. They are still tied there."

"He is a slow-witted . . ."

"Ah, do not speak of your father-in-law-to-be like that, my son. Be patient."

That same sun, when the shadows were already long and thin across the ground, Little Redbird left her father's lodge forever and walked over to Sun Runner's lodge, carrying a bundle of her things. The two were married in two suns, and Sun Runner built a fine lodge for her.

The snows came and went and the people traveled and hunted, fought with Pawnee and other tribes. Sun Runner forgot all about the things that Old Lodge had told him, until one day, when the people were camped on the Little Powder at the place where it runs into the Powder River, Bear Heart came to his son's lodge with bad news.

"Old Lodge is dying," he said. "Come."

Little Redbird, who was heavy with child, nodded. Sun Runner went with his father to Old Lodge's house.

Many people stood outside the lodge with long faces. They all stepped to one side as Sun Runner approached. He was much respected, for he had fought many battles, struck many coups, was a member of the Kit Fox Society, and had a wife full with child.

"Old Lodge asks to speak to you, Sun Runner," said a famous warrior called Alights On The Cloud. He lifted the lodge flap and Sun Runner went in alone.

The lodge smelled of sweat and boiled medicine roots. Wool Woman, his aunt, was there, with Corn Woman and Little Redbird's mother, One-Legged

Crane. They looked like shadows in the lodge and were very quiet. In the corner was a medicine man who chanted in soft whispers. This one was Old Porcupine, a good doctor to the people.

Old Lodge lay almost naked on thick buffalo robes, his body bathed in sweat, his eyes glittering in the firelight, like sun-stones. He looked very frail and weak. Sun Runner could see the bones of his ribs, and his neck was very thin and the skin wrinkled like the throat of a lizard.

"You have come, my son," said the old man, his voice weak, high-pitched. "Sit. I will talk some before I die."

Sun Runner felt a lump form in his throat.

He sat next to Old Lodge. The old man lifted a shaking hand, put it on Sun Runner's arm. His palm was warm with fever. Wool Woman started to sob, but Corn Woman put her hand over the woman's mouth, then took it away.

"I am very sick, son," said Old Lodge, breathy from exhaustion. "The *Ho-ho-ta-ma-itsi-hyo-ist,* the Ground People, shot me with invisible arrows. I think it must have happened when I went to the spring. I think I was not thinking right and I jumped across the little trickle of water where it comes out of the rocks and the spirits who live in the ground shot me. I was careless. I took some presents and laid them by the spring, but it was too late. The arrows stayed in me, and I am dying. Pretty fast now, I think."

"No," murmured Sun Runner.

"Listen. I am giving to you a pipe. Corn Woman, give your son the pipe I have for him."

Corn Woman handed Sun Runner a fine straight pipe,

decorated with hawk's feathers, beads, a Crow scalp-lock, and painted with sacred symbols. Sun Runner bowed his head, sat quiet, with the pipe across his lap.

Old Lodge moved his hand to the pipe, lifted it from Sun Runner's lap. He touched the young man on each shoulder with the pipe, then put it back on Sun Runner's lap.

"I have smoked the pipe and now my good medicine is yours," said Old Lodge. "When you smoke it, think of me. Think of what I told you many snows past. Do you remember?"

"I remember, old father."

"Soon you will have a big fight with the Pawnee. You will kill some, strike many coups. Some of our good people will be killed and there will be a long sadness from this. After that, you will see the soldier-people who have no darkness to their skins. You must not let them capture you. You must stay away from them."

"Then, I will not die?" Sun Runner asked.

The old man's throat made a sound like the medicine rattle and his chest strained to bring in breath. The doctor stopped praying and waved a hawk's wing across Old Lodge's face.

"I see the bright trail," said Old Lodge with his last breath. His body shuddered as the spirit left it. The women rocked backward on their legs and trilled their shrill keening cries.

"Go," said Old Porcupine to Sun Runner. "Go quickly."

Bewildered, Sun Runner got up and stumbled from the lodge, grief-stricken, the pipe slippery in his clammy hands.

Bear Heart touched his son's shoulder.

"He has gone, then," he said.

Sun Runner nodded numbly, staggered toward his own lodge, fighting back the tears, his throat aching as if he had swallowed fire.

Sun Runner was angry. He had missed the fight with the Pawnee when many brave men had been killed. Alights On The Cloud, who by then was called Iron Shirt because he wore armor, had died, an arrow shot into his eye by the Pawnee they called *Ta-wi-ta-da-hila-sa*, Carrying The Shield In Front. Now, a snow later, those deaths had not been avenged. Sun Runner's son, Gray Wolf, was into his second summer and Little Redbird was already teasing him about making another baby for their lodge. There was snow on the ground, the sky gray with clouds, and they had made love, but always the blood had come afterward.

"Do you not want Gray Wolf to have a baby sister, one as pretty as me?" Little Redbird chided her husband. Her braids hung over her shoulders, the tightly woven strands interlaced with beadwork and pieces of brightly colored cloth. Her cheeks were daubed lightly with vermilion. Sun Runner ached when he looked at her, ached in muscle and bone and flesh.

"Woman, you are without shame. There are other matters more important than making a baby."

"Gray Plover, the wife of Red Tracks, already is about to give light."

"I do not want to hear of Red Tracks or his ugly wife, Gray Plover." Secretly, he was glad that Red Tracks had not married Golden Quail. She was now the wife of

Hawk Diving, and Gray Plover had turned into a nagging magpie, grown fat and lazy like a she-bear in the season of the berries turning black. "Alights On The Cloud was a fine, generous man, brave, with a kind heart. I thought the iron shirt would protect him. I thought his medicine was very strong."

"So, you worry about your own death, my husband?"

"No!" he shouted. "I want to avenge the man. I want to kill Pawnee!"

He was sorry he spoke out in anger, and his face darkened with blood. He rose from his blankets and stormed out of the lodge, the sound of Little Redbird's weeping strong in his ears.

"What of the talk last snow to send the pipe about?" Sun Runner asked Rope Earrings and Bear Heart, when he saw them.

"In a little while, when the snows melt," said Rope Earrings, "Little Robe will carry the pipe to the northern Cheyennes."

"Yellow Nose will carry the pipe to the southern Cheyennes," said Bear Heart.

"Haw!" exclaimed Sun Runner. "Talk. It is almost spring now and I have heard no criers, seen no pipe-bearer."

"In two sleeps, we move to Beaver Creek," said Rope Earrings. "But go you to the lodge of Walks At Night. He wants to give you a present."

"Me? Why?"

"He says you bring him great honor, have given him a fine grandson, little Gray Wolf."

Sun Runner did not trust Rope Earrings. He was

often joking and it may be he was pulling Sun Runner's hair this sun.

"I have heard this too," said Bear Heart to his son. "Go. See what Walks At Night will give you."

Sun Runner called Walks At Night from his lodge. The man, his hair snowy from forty winters, came out, dressed in beaded buckskins, his hair rubbed with aromatic leaves, an eagle feather dangling behind his ear. He carried a rope and a halter in his hand.

"Oh, I have a present for you, Sun Runner. Come, we will walk."

They strode to the pony herd, and Walks At Night spoke to one of the young herders.

"Catch my white horse," he said. "Fetch it to me."

The boy, Little Owl, took the rope and halter, raced off. Sun Runner's heart made pump-thunder in his ears. Soon, the boy returned, leading the fine white horse. There was no black on it, no other color. It was white as a cloud.

"Take this horse. It is a good horse, very strong, with big lungs. Look at his legs. Soon we will fight the Pawnee. We will avenge Iron Shirt."

Sun Runner took the rope, worked it off the horse's neck, grabbed the halter. His heart swelled in his chest.

"You give me this gift," he said. "I accept it. It is a fine horse. Why do you talk of the Pawnee? I have not seen the pipe-bearer."

"He will come when we are on Beaver Creek at the South Platte's mouth. All the soldier bands will gather there."

"Who says these things?"

"A runner came in after the sun went to sleep last

night. He sleeps now, this Dog Soldier who is called War Bonnet."

"I know him. He is very brave. I have heard talk of him."

"You will lead the Kit Fox Soldiers. They will all be able to see you on this fine white horse."

"I give thanks to my father-in-law for this gift." Sun Runner mounted the horse and rode him off toward the horizon. The hooves crunched through frozen snow, kicked up clumps of ice in the prairie wallows. The horse was strong, had good wind for running. It would make a fine war-horse, he thought.

He halted the horse far from the village, sat its back as the animal blew steam-smoke through its nostrils. He rubbed its withers, spoke to it.

The words of Old Lodge came back to him, then. He had forgotten them, bundled them deep in his memory like sacred things kept hidden under many blankets.

He wondered, then, if he would see the pale soldier-people soon. Old Lodge had told him of the gift of the white horse. He also had warned him of the fight with the Pawnee. Now, part of what Old Lodge foretold had come true. The white horse was under him and there was talk of revenge against the Pawnee.

Sun Runner looked to the sky and drew a deep breath.

The sky was empty, but the gray clouds moved away and the sun came to life, blazed down on the snow. Sun Runner looked down and saw his shadow and the horse's shadow. There was no other shadow.

No hawk flew over him.

CHAPTER SEVENTEEN

Little Robe, *Ski-o-mah*, of the Northern Cheyennes, carried the pipe that spring to all the camps along the South Platte. Yellow Nose, *O-itan*, of the Southern Cheyennes, carried the pipe to those far-flung camps on the Republican, the Smoky Hill, and the Arkansas Rivers. Sun Runner's band, now under Little Wolf's chieftainship, was part of the main village set at the mouth of Beaver Creek. He stayed in the huge lodge that was the meeting place for each of the soldier bands.

For several suns, he had listened in anguish to the pleas of those related to warriors killed before the last snow in the fight with the Pawnees.

"Take pity on my son and my daughters," wailed Blue Shell Woman, whose husband had been slain and cut open like a buffalo calf.

Earrings' wife was there too, and told how the brother of Iron Shirt wanted to die after Iron Shirt was shot through the eye by a left-handed Pawnee. Bald-Faced Bull and Kiowa Woman told more tales of that fatal summer hunt when the Pawnees swarmed at them out of a great dust cloud—which the Cheyennes thought was only a great herd of buffalo running—and killed many of them and took scalps.

The mourners brought many presents to the soldiers

and Sun Runner himself was given seven horses. He learned from Little Robe that messengers had been sent to the Burnt Thigh Lakota, to the Arapahoes, the Kiowas and Apaches.

"They will be offered the pipe to join us as we fight the Pawnee and destroy them," said Little Robe, in council. "And we have taken the pipe to the Crow and some of them are coming. Go now, all of you to the place near *Sav-an-i-yo-he* (Shawnee Creek, a tributary of the Arickaree Fork of the Republican River), and we will make a fight with the Pawnee."

The lodges were struck, and many large bands of Cheyenne journeyed to the great camp on the headwaters of the Republican. There, a great medicine lodge was erected and Sun Runner's Kit Fox Soldiers conducted all the ceremonies, which were long and torturous. He, like the other Kit Fox Soldiers, suffered as much as the dancers. He, too, had to go without food or drink during the ceremony.

Wood, *Ka-mahk',* and Two Thighs, *Nish-i-no-mah',* two of the Fox Soldier band, made talk on the last day of the ceremony.

"Now," said Wood, "this is the last day of the dance. We are not far from the country of the Pawnee. It is time for us to choose scouts and send them out to find the Pawnee camp."

"Who shall we choose?" asked Two Thighs. "There is Mad Wolf over there. Let us choose him for one."

"Shall we also choose Sun Runner?" asked Wood. "He is pretty brave and pretty cunning. Let us ask him if he will scout the Pawnee camp."

The two chiefs pointed to Mad Wolf and Sun Runner,

who were sitting on the grasses some distance away. Fox Soldiers strode up to them and asked them if they would act as scouts for the Cheyenne.

"I do not think so," said Sun Runner. "The honor is too great for such a poor man as this one."

"Come," said Hawk Diving, suppressing a smile. "You have been chosen."

"No, I do not accept this honor."

"Get him," said Makes Thunder.

Since it was considered impolite that a man should seem anxious to be honored as one chosen to go as a scout on so important a search, Sun Runner hung back, resisted. He tried to escape, but his friends chased him down and caught him. They held his arms and pushed him up to the shady place where the leaders of the Fox Soldiers were sitting.

"Sit on the blanket with Mad Wolf," gruffed Makes Thunder.

Sun Runner sat down. He slumped, trying not to show his pride at being one of those chosen for such a great honor.

"Sit here for a while," said Wood, "until we bring in those others who will sit with you."

The soldiers searched the huge camp and found War Bonnet, *Ka-ko-hy-i-si-nih',* in his lodge and brought him up to the place in the shade. They brought Tall Bull, *Hotu-a-e-hka-ash-tait,* Starving Elk, *Mohk'-sta-wo-ums-ts,* and Little Wolf, *Oh'-kum-hka-kit.* Then, Wood and Two Thighs told the soldiers to bring up the Kiowa, Dirt On The Nose, and when they had the men they wanted sitting on the blanket, Wood stood among the Fox Soldiers and spoke to them.

"Now, my friends, you know what the feeling is in this camp. We want to find the enemy. You men have been chosen to do this because we think you are good men. We want you to go ahead and do your best. You must remember that you are not going out to count coups, nor to take scalps nor horses. But you are going to find out where the enemy is, and then bring back this news to camp. I will go with you to see that you do what you are told. You can go now and get your horses and start on down the river. I will go ahead and stop at a certain place, where we will all meet this afternoon."

Sun Runner went and caught up one of his horses, a small, rangy pinto with good strong legs and a deep chest, then rode to his lodge. He went inside to get his weapons. Little Redbird and Gray Wolf were playing together in the cool shadows of the lodge.

"I have been chosen as a scout for the Fox Soldiers," he told her.

"You give me much pride. My heart soars like the eagle."

Gray Wolf looked at his father with wide, trusting eyes. He was a chubby youngster of four summers now. His face was smeared with dirt and he had a bowl full of lizards and bugs that he was torturing with glee.

"We will find the Pawnee camp," said Sun Runner. "I go with Wood."

"Gray Wolf and I will sing little songs for you," said his wife.

Sun Runner left, joined the other scouts. He now had a fine saddle and a knife made of metal. Many of the braves had rifles. He carried a small one that he had taken from a Snake he had killed. It loaded from the front of the barrel and made a big hole. He had a small amount of powder and lead, plenty of flintstones to make the spark that fired the powder in the little bowl. It had once been a longer rifle, he knew, but someone had cut it off short. It was heavy, but he liked to shoot it.

They met Wood at the top of a hill late in the sun's path across the skies. Some who were not chosen had followed the scouts and rode in. Red Tracks and three others sat their ponies, knowing they had not been ordered out.

"What shall we do with these?" asked War Bonnet.

"Well, we cannot send them back," said Wood. "Let them go along. Let us now go down to the river and take a bath and start in the cool of the evening and travel at night."

They all went down to the river and swam. There were many buffalo there because it was right after *O-ssi'-owah-tut',* the May moon, near the moon when the buffalo bulls are rutting, *Hivi-uits-i'-shi.* The grass was up tall and green and the sun burned hot on the earth. The bulls near the river were fighting, grunting like bears and dashing about looking for conquests. The bulls at that time would charge anything, and the men had to be careful.

Sun Runner lay on the bank, his naked body wet and glistening in the sun. Some of the other Cheyennes sogged up to him and lay down, enjoying themselves. Suddenly, a bull charged out of the brush and headed straight for them. His head was wrapped in grapevines and he trailed long tendrils behind him. Sun Runner leaped up, along with the others, and they scattered as the rutting bull lowered his head and tried to butt them. Sun Runner leaped out of the bull's way just a heartbeat or two from being struck and the animal lumbered into the river, sending a huge muddy wake over the other swimmers.

Tall Bull rode into the timber while the others were making ready to leave. He killed a fat cow, called to the warriors. They cut up the cow into choice pieces, tied the meat to their ponies.

"We will ride until the sun makes the shadows longest, then stop and cook this meat," said Wood. The party of scouts traveled until the sun was about to go to bed, then stopped, made a fire. It was dark when they finished eating, and they rode much of the night, stopped at one place to rest, and at another to sleep. They rode on most of the next sun into the long shadows of afternoon.

"There are wolves," said Sun Runner, pointing to the horizon ahead. "They are running away."

The scouts all galloped ahead, found a freshly killed buffalo carcass. In it was a single arrow.

"Pawnee," said Tall Bull, leaning down to pull the shaft from the animal's neck.

They rode on, through the prairie valley, saw many carcasses scattered here and there, and skeletons of buffalo.

"There are many killed," said Wood. "We are close to the Pawnee camp." He sent Warbonnet and Tall Bull ahead to scout and they rode to the top of a hill. Soon, they returned, riding hard.

"We saw two or three people going over that far hill over there. Probably the Pawnee camp is down below," said Warbonnet.

"You are probably right," said Wood. "Well, we have found what we came looking for. Look at all these fresh carcasses around us. Let us return to the village and tell them what we have found."

When the scouting party returned to camp, Wood sent the others back, in single file, and rode well to the rear. The men howled like wolves, raced their mounts into the village. The people shouted, and men began to catch up their horses. They saddled up for war, painted their faces, set out their war medicines. In the center of the camp, many heaped up a great pile of buffalo chips on which to count coup. Many of the young men mounted up and rode around the camp singing their war songs, throwing their shields up in the air, and charged at the pile of buffalo chips with lances and warclubs.

"What did you find? Where are the Pawnee?" asked the hot-blooded young braves of Warbonnet.

"My friend Wood will tell you that," replied Warbonnet.

By the time Wood arrived, the camp was in a frenzy. He sent a crier around the camp to call in all the soldier societies for a ceremonial march on the slope above the village. Sun Runner unsaddled his pinto and caught up the white horse that Walks At Night had given him. He painted the sacred signs on the animal, painted himself for war.

All of the warrior societies made the ceremonial march on horseback: the Crooked Lances, Dog Soldiers, Kit Fox Soldiers, and the Bowstrings. Each man sang his personal war song and the people stood in

awe of this orderly procession. Afterward, before they
could return to their lodges, the men ordered boys to
wash the sacred paint from their horses. The river filled
with ponies as old men and boys carried out the orders
of the warriors. Sun Runner removed his shield and
warbonnet and put them back in their cases. He put the
cover on his lance and carried these things back to his
lodge.

That night Sun Runner played with his son, Gray
Wolf, while Little Redbird finished making new moccasins for her men. Her hands were trembling as she
worked the bone awl through the softened hide.

"Are there many Pawnee?" she asked.

"I do not know. Maybe."

"I fear for my man."

"Do not fear, woman. My medicine is strong." He
cuffed Gray Wolf playfully, sent the boy tumbling into a
pile of robes. The boy laughed and struggled like an
overturned turtle for several beats of the heart. Sun
Runner dragged him out of the pile, threw him upon
his back like a cape. The boy pulled on his father's hair,
covered Sun Runner's eyes with tiny hands. Sun Runner shrugged his shoulders, gave the boy a ride on his
back as he hopped around the lodge.

"I had a bad dream while you were gone," said Little
Redbird.

"What was this dream?"

"I do not remember. But it was bad. I have fear.
Much fear."

"That is what women have," he said, and he put the
boy aside and crawled into his blankets. Gray Wolf tod-
dled over to his mother and played with a moccasin

until he heard Sun Runner's snoring. Little Redbird put away her things and held the boy, rocked him in her arms as she sang a lullaby to him. After Gray Wolf fell asleep, she put him in his blankets and crawled into her husband's bed. She put a hand on his chest and snuggled into the warmth of his shoulder. But it was a long time before she slept.

CHAPTER EIGHTEEN

Early during the next sun, the Cheyenne village moved downriver to set up another camp close to the Pawnees. The women spent all day fixing up the lodges, building platforms to keep the food from the wolves and coyotes, finishing last minute chores. After the sun went to sleep, the entire village started out for the Pawnee camp, the men riding their war-horses, the women following behind, on foot. Gray Wolf, and all the smaller children, rode on travois.

They slept in the open that night and marched again early the following morning. When they were close to the Pawnee camp, the women and children, the old ones, all hid behind a hill while the men rode away to begin preparations for battle. Sun Runner looked at his wife and son, winced to see their faces so stony, and rode off with his warrior society, his stomach knotted tight as a drumhead.

He stopped, with the other warriors, and began to unwrap his medicine bundle. He sang his personal song as the sacred hat was placed atop a bed of sage stems and an arrow was taken from the sacred bundle and given to Wooden Leg. This one sang the arrow song, danced, thrust the arrow toward the Pawnee camp. Sun Runner and the others stamped their feet in time to the singing and jabbed his lance toward the enemy, shoved his shield at them until the four songs were finished. All the men whooped as Wooden Leg returned the arrow to Rock Forehead, keeper of the sacred bundle.

Sun Runner mounted his white horse, set the lance in its sheath, hung his shield from the saddle. He strung his bow, drew an arrow from his quiver. He was ready.

Then, a thing happened that made his stomach turn over, boil bile up into his throat. Big Head and his braves started riding toward the Pawnee camp, hoping to be first to count coup and take a scalp. This was against the unspoken rule and broke the medicine of the arrows and the hat.

Red Tracks saw this, too, and cried out in anguish. He looked at Sun Runner then.

"Why do you look at me?" Sun Runner asked.

"I thought of another sun when the medicine was broken," said the older man. "It will go bad for us now."

Sun Runner glared at Red Tracks, then turned away, not wishing to spoil things with his hatred.

The cry was given and the Cheyennes charged on their horses toward the Pawnee camp. The women and children broke from cover and raced after the men, were swallowed up in dust.

The Pawnees were not there. They had moved their camp. The Cheyenne galloped upstream and down, searching for them. Soon, Big Head came riding up, waving a fresh scalp.

"The camp is over that hill there," he shouted. "Go slow. There are many Pawnee."

Sun Runner kicked his horse hard, the bloodlust strong in him. The Cheyenne charged over the hill.

The Pawnee were ready for them. Their women and children and horses were all down in the creek, protected by its high banks, and the enemy warriors were behind hastily erected breastworks, waiting.

With his warbonnet rattling in the breeze, Sun Runner charged toward a bunch of Pawnees who were out in the open. He nocked an arrow, drew his bow. Dark lines filled the air in front of him as a flight of Pawnee arrows winged toward him. He shouted a blood-curdling cry and picked out a target. He loosed the arrow, saw it arc toward a defiant Pawnee who was jumping up and down, shouting. The arrow struck the man in the groin and he fell to the ground.

Sun Runner rode for him, jerked his lance free of its sheath. He struck the man in the head as he rode by, shouted his triumph at counting coup. Many Cheyenne saw this brave act and shouted in praise of Sun Runner.

Cheyenne warriors flanked the breastworks then, and Pawnee braves spilled out of their hiding places and began to run around madly, shooting and shouting. A cloud of dust rose in the air and the ground turned bloody as the two opposing forces clashed like two great herds of buffalo coming together.

Some of the Pawnees ran to the creek and climbed on horses. A dozen of them closed one flank, and cut through a pack of Cheyennes, striking coup and shooting two braves from their ponies. Then the Pawnees rode out onto the prairie, seeking the high ground.

Sun Runner saw Bear Heart and Rope Earrings, along with Makes Thunder and Red Tracks, wheel their horses to chase after these Pawnees.

"Wait," Sun Runner shouted. "I will go with you." He

drew an arrow from his quiver, caught up with his father and the others. The Pawnees ran zigzag patterns well ahead of them, their horses fresh, still wet from being belly-deep in the creek.

The sun beat down on Sun Runner. Horse and rider cast a racing shadow on the earth. Heat shimmered on the knoll where the Pawnee were headed and Sun Runner thought he saw the silhouettes of men on horseback beyond the crest. An odd feeling gripped him. He wondered, for the skip of a heartbeat, if the Pawnee braves were leading them into a trap.

"Hell of a noise over yonder," said Lance Corporal James Bellaugh.

"Injuns huntin' buffalo, likely," said the white scout, Earl Poston, attached, most recently, to the Sixth Infantry out of Fort Laramie.

The lieutenant, a man named Fleming, rode up beside Captain Edward Johnson.

"Sir," said Fleming, "should we reconnoiter?"

"We'll see what's going on, Lieutenant," said Johnson, with dry, ill-concealed sarcasm. "That's what this patrol is all about."

"Yes, sir."

"Poston." The captain flicked his hand to bring the scout up.

Poston swore and caught up with the officer.

"Yeah?"

"Take the point."

Poston said nothing. He didn't have to. A moment later, they all saw the Pawnee warriors break over the crest of the knoll, scatter along the ridge, their bodies gleaming in the bright sunlight.

"Shit," said the scout.

"Whoa!" Johnson called out. He held up a hand and the dozen troopers, the lieutenant, all reined in, skidding their horses to a halt.

No one spoke. They all heard the yells and screams beyond the knoll. The *pop-pop-pop* of rifle and pistol fire floated through the silence. Dust billowed over the hill.

Fleming rattled his saber. The soldiers touched their hands to rifle stocks, awaiting an order from their captain.

"Cap'n," said Poston, "I'd stay out of this was I you. Them's Pawnee up yonder and they's somethin' real bad got them riled. Cheyenne, I reckon."

"Christ," muttered the captain.

Sun Runner topped the hill, heeled his horse over hard to run down a Pawnee. The Pawnee sang a death song, hugged the back of his horse. Sun Runner shot him in the side, saw the arrow *thung* into the ribs, vibrate as the blood spilled from the wounded man's side. He gave a shout of triumph, then saw the men on horseback through the shimmering ghost waters that the sun made.

The Pawnee rode toward the soldiers, still alive.

He taunted Sun Runner, made an obscene gesture. Sun Runner gave chase.

"Son, do not go there," shouted his father, Bear Heart.

"Come back!" Rope Earrings yelled.

The other Cheyenne stopped their horses, looked toward the soldiers.

Sun Runner caught up to the Pawnee, struck him hard with his bow. Once, twice. The Pawnee slipped from his pony, hit the ground, skidded. Sun Runner jerked hard on the ropes of his horse's bridle and stopped. He leaped from the white horse's back, drew his knife with the sharp metal blade.

The Pawnee tried to get up.

Sun Runner plunged his knife into the brave's throat. Blood exploded over his hand. He wrenched the knife free. The Pawnee crumpled. His eyes frosted over with the glaze of death and his spirit left him.

The soldiers walked their horses in closer.

Sun Runner saw them coming, saw their colorless faces, their shadowy eyes.

He grabbed the dead Pawnee by both braids, jerked his head up. He slashed into the scalp, cut off half his hair, pulled it free of the clinging meat. He grunted in triumph, shook the bloody scalp as he held it high for all to see.

He mounted his horse, made the animal strut back and forth as the soldiers kept walking their horses toward him. He had heard of the white people all his life, but he had never seen one before. These were soldier-people, all dressed the same, except for one.

"Come back," called Bear Heart, and his voice sounded far away to Sun Runner.

Sun Runner turned his horse then, wanting to get back into the battle with the Pawnee.

He heard the *crack* of the rifle, then the roar-sound like a thunder, slapping his ears. He felt the sting-smack of the ball as it struck him between the shoulder blades. The earth tilted and the sky spun. He gasped for breath, tried to cry out with the pain and the shock.

"Poston," growled the captain, "why in hell did you do that?"

"I hate a sumbitch takin' scalp like that."

"Men," said Johnson, "if that Cheyenne drops, we'll be up to our brassards in Indians. Walk your mounts. Fall back. Don't arm yourselves unless I give a direct order."

"Yes, sir!" barked Fleming.

The soldiers began to back their horses. Poston held his rifle across the pommel of his saddle, at the ready. He scowled, wondered why the Cheyenne didn't go down. He saw the shot go home, knew that it was bound to be fatal.

The lead ball did not pass through Sun Runner's body. As he rode back toward the knoll, he heard his mind singing his death song. He had no voice. Bear Heart did not know his son was shot, because he gave a sign and rode off after Rope Earrings and the others.

Sun Runner saw the earth swimming before him, but he was in shock. He came upon two Pawnee horses, grabbed their halters by the ropes, led them back toward the place where the women and children were gathered. Many Cheyenne saw him ride through them, bullets and arrows whizzing all around him. None noticed the small hole in his back, the streak of blood along his spine.

Little Redbird and Gray Wolf ran out to meet him. He handed her the ropes and she nodded. Through the paint on her husband's face, she saw the pain, the beads of sweat. She put Gray Wolf on one pony, jumped up on the other.

Sun Runner turned his horse to the north. Little Redbird fell behind. She gave a small cry and touched a hand to her husband's back. Her fingers stuck to the blood. She pulled her hand away, began to sob.

Gray Wolf, delighted at being on the pony, grinned wide.

"Where do we go, my husband?" asked a shaking Little Redbird, her voice quavering.

Sun Runner sucked in a breath, found his voice one last time.

"We go home," he said. "We will be the people again. We will be as we once were, free as the hawk."

Little Redbird sobbed deep.

The Cheyenne watched them ride away, and wondered. They all saw the red hawk float over them and heard its shrill cry.

Screeee! Screeee!

EPILOG

I, Woven Rug, the grandson of Alights On The Cloud, who was also known as Iron Shirt, have told this story, because the darkest days of the Cheyenne came to pass after Sun Runner was killed that day our people fought the Pawnee. No one saw his death scaffold. No one knows where he and Little Redbird and Gray Wolf went after that.

But there were those who said they saw him after that, at Ash Hollow, and at Sand Creek. Some said they saw him at Beecher Island and at the battle of Summit Springs, and at Wounded Knee. Many spoke of seeing him, and the hawk's shadow flying across the battlefield on the Rosebud and at the Little Big Horn.

There is even talk in my lifetime, even after all the old memories are gone, dead with the minds of the people who lived those times.

The miners and the white settlers, who came after Custer, often spoke of seeing three Indians on a hilltop, or riding through the morning mist, long after the war drums had gone silent, long after the grass had grown tall over the valley of the Little Big Horn.

And, sometimes, the whites said they could hear a prayer chant floating across the hills after the sun went over the mountains.

Some say Sun Runner is still out there, roaming the

Black Hills, Little Redbird at his side, Gray Wolf on his pony bringing up the rear.

I have been there, seen these visions. I have heard the rattling sound of wind in a warbonnet's eagle feathers and seen the grass wave in certain places as though ghosts were riding through it, leaving streaks, wide channels of bent stalks in their wake.

Now, I sit out there sometimes, alone, and listen, and wonder. In the hawking cries of the crow, is there the far-off note of a Cheyenne war cry? Or is this only an illusion?

At times, there is the little thunder of moccasins running through a place where Cheyenne lodges once stood, and the old Lakotas I know from the Rosebud and the Pine Ridge reservations go there and say it is Sun Runner come back to the hunting grounds, to the place of his great medicine.

"His spirit was strong," said one man to me, who remembers the stories his father told him, who remembers the proud days of the Cheyenne when they rode with the Lakota and they ran over Custer and left his tattered battle flags flapping in the wind.

"He is gone forever," said another. "Dead."

Yet, who's to say he is not still there, that he will not be there forever? Who's to say his spirit is not stronger than any other and that he does not still run faster than his shadow, faster than the sun?

ABOUT THE AUTHOR

Jory Sherman has been a magazine editor, a teacher of creative writing, and most frequently, a columnist for a variety of newspapers. He is the author of dozens of novels, primarily in the Western genre, under his own name and several pseudonyms.